meeting with

my brother

WEATHERHEAD BOOKS ON ASIA

WEATHERHEAD BOOKS ON ASIA

Weatherhead East Asian Institute, Columbia University

LITERATURE

David Der-wei Wang, Editor

Ye Zhaoyan, *Nanjing 1937: A Love Story*, translated by Michael Berry (2003)

Oda Makato, *The Breaking Jewel*, translated by Donald Keene (2003)

Han Shaogong, *A Dictionary of Maqiao*, translated by Julia Lovell (2003)

Takahashi Takako, *Lonely Woman*, translated by Maryellen Toman Mori (2004)

Chen Ran, *A Private Life*, translated by John Howard-Gibbon (2004)

Eileen Chang, *Written on Water*, translated by Andrew F. Jones (2004)

Writing Women in Modern China: The Revolutionary Years, 1936–1976, edited by Amy D. Dooling (2005)

Han Bangqing, *The Sing-song Girls of Shanghai*, first translated by Eileen Chang, revised and edited by Eva Hung (2005)

Loud Sparrows: Contemporary Chinese Short-Shorts, translated and edited by Aili Mu, Julie Chiu, and Howard Goldblatt (2006)

Hiratsuka Raichō, *In the Beginning, Woman Was the Sun*, translated by Teruko Craig (2006)

Zhu Wen, *I Love Dollars and Other Stories of China*, translated by Julia Lovell (2007)

Kim Sowŏl, *Azaleas: A Book of Poems*, translated by David McCann (2007)

Wang Anyi, *The Song of Everlasting Sorrow: A Novel of Shanghai*, translated by Michael Berry with Susan Chan Egan (2008)

Ch'oe Yun, *There a Petal Silently Falls: Three Stories by Ch'oe Yun*, translated by Bruce and Ju-Chan Fulton (2008)

Inoue Yasushi, *The Blue Wolf: A Novel of the Life of Chinggis Khan*, translated by Joshua A. Fogel (2009)

Anonymous, *Courtesans and Opium: Romantic Illusions of the Fool of Yangzhou*, translated by Patrick Hanan (2009)

Cao Naiqian, *There's Nothing I Can Do When I Think of You Late at Night*, translated by John Balcom (2009)

Park Wan-suh, *Who Ate Up All the Shinga? An Autobiographical Novel*, translated by Yu Young-nan and Stephen J. Epstein (2009)

Yi T'aejun, *Eastern Sentiments*, translated by Janet Poole (2009)

Hwang Sunwŏn, *Lost Souls: Stories*, translated by Bruce and Ju-Chan Fulton (2009)

Kim Sŏk-pŏm, *The Curious Tale of Mandogi's Ghost*, translated by Cindi Textor (2010)

(continued on page 95)

meeting with my brother

A NOVELLA

YI MUN-YOL

TRANSLATED BY
Heinz Insu Fenkl
with Yoosup Chang

COLUMBIA UNIVERSITY PRESS   *New York*

This publication has been supported by the Richard W. Weatherhead
Publication Fund of the Weatherhead East Asian Institute, Columbia
University.

This book is published with the support of the Literature Translation Institute
of Korea (LTI Korea).

COLUMBIA UNIVERSITY PRESS
Publishers Since 1893
New York   Chichester, West Sussex
cup.columbia.edu

Library of Congress Cataloging-in-Publication Data

Names: Yi, Mun-yŏl, 1948- author. | Fenkl, Heinz Insu, 1960- translator. |
   Chang, Yoosup, translator.
Title: Meeting with my brother : a novella / Yi Mun-yŏl ; translated by Heinz
   Insu Fenkl with Yoosup Chang.
Other titles: Au waŭi mannam. English
Description: New York : Columbia University Press, 2017. | Series:
   Weatherhead books on Asia
Identifiers: LCCN 2016043400 (print) | LCCN 2017005104 (ebook) | ISBN
   9780231178648 (cloth : alk. paper) | ISBN 9780231544672 (electronic)
Subjects: LCSH: Brothers—North Korea—Fiction. | Families—North
   Korea—Fiction. | Korean War, 1950-1953—Fiction. | GSAFD: War stories.
Classification: LCC PL992.9.M83 A913 2017 (print) | LCC PL992.9.M83
   (ebook) | DDC 895.73/4—dc23
LC record available at https://lccn.loc.gov/2016043400

Printed in the United States of America

COVER IMAGE: © NOH SUNTAG, RED HOUSE II, GIVE AND TAKE
#24, 2006

COVER DESIGN: CHANG JAE LEE

contents

introduction

When I was a reader, a novel was like a haven where I could escape from reality. After I became a novelist, I began to think about what role my novels should serve . . . I thought about a writer's sense of mission or redemption.

—Yi Mun-yol

I

Yi Mun-yol was born in Seoul in 1948, two years before the outbreak of the Korean War. His father, Yi Weon-cheol, an intellectual who had been jailed for anticolonial activities against the Japanese, was a member of the Korean Worker's Party. He abandoned his family and defected to the North during the war, leaving them forever branded as the family of a traitor. And yet, despite this terrible stigma of being the son of a communist—or perhaps, ironically, because of it—Yi Mun-yol was to become the most prominent and most socially significant literary figure of post-1980s Korea. There is no other writer whose work addresses such a broad spectrum of psychological, cultural, political, and historical themes, and no other writer whose work offers a stylistic range that encompasses much of the history of modern Korean literature following the end of the Japanese colonial era.

The Korean War displaced and fragmented more than ten million families because the unusually rapid pace of the military activity required multiple evacuations. Those who were known to have family members who were communist were often killed by the military, the police, or vengeful civilians. For the safety of the family, Yi's mother kept herself and her five children constantly moving, often late at night when neighbors would not see them, and this continued every two or three years until the South Korean government made a fixed address mandatory. So, after the country's ultimate division in 1953, Yi spent most of his childhood living with one relative then another, in various cities like Yeongcheon, Yeongyang, and Andong, finally settling in Miryang in 1959. There, he enrolled in middle school but dropped out after only six months. Later, he also dropped out of high school after attending only one year and then spent the next three years moving from one odd job to the next in the Busan area along the eastern coast. That he was able to pass the diploma test and enter the Seoul National University School of Education after his troubled childhood and disrupted education is a testament to his determination and hard work. By American standards, Yi's is a kind of Horatio Alger story, an autodidact pulling himself up by his bootstraps after enduring the school of hard knocks. And yet in 1970 Yi would even drop out of prestigious Seoul National University (the epitome of success and status by Korean standards) before he had completed his degree. In Korea, Yi's life has a heroic and nearly mythic quality, as he was able to overcome terrible disadvantages and repeated setbacks to achieve literary fame.

Yi married in 1973 and completed his mandatory military service in 1976. In interviews, he mentions that he had considered becoming a lawyer while he was at Seoul National, a career move that would have redeemed his family to some degree and helped with their finances. But he dreamed of being a writer and devoted much of his energy to being an active member of a literary club. In 1978 he won the *Maeil News* Spring Literary Contest, and the prize helped land him a job as a journalist. Then, in 1979, he won the *Dong A Daily* Spring Literary Contest with his story "Saehagok," which brought him national attention. Later that year, he won the Today's Writer Award, given by one of Korea's major publishers, Minumsa, for his first novel, *Son of Man*, securing his position as a national literary star. Since then Yi has won just about every major literary award Korea has to offer: the Dongin Literary Prize for "Golden Phoenix" (also translated as "Garuda") in 1982, the Korean Literature Prize for his magnum opus *Hail to the Emperor* in 1983, the Jungang Culture Grand Prize for *Age of Heroes* in 1984, and the much-coveted Yi Sang Literary prize for his novella *Our Twisted Hero* in 1987. He also won the Hyundae Award in 1992, the Twenty-First-Century Literature Prize in 1998, the Ho-Am Prize in 1999, the National Academy of Arts Award in 2009, and the Dongni Literature Prize in 2012.

One quality that made Yi worthy of so many literary awards is his unflinching ability to confront thematic, formal, and political challenges in his writing. Korean readers—both the general reading public and the literary intelligentsia known as the *mundan*—are partial to debate and controversy. Since modern Korean literature was born out of the Japanese colonial era and developed through the oppressive administrations of military dictators, the role of the writer has always been one fraught with a high degree of moral and ethical responsibility (it is only in relatively recent times that the kind of commercial publishing familiar in the West has become the dominant system). In this climate, in which a literary work can serve as a seed crystal for instigating social and political dialogue, Yi has consistently confronted difficult and charged themes.

For example, his first novel, *Son of Man*, could pass for a mystery, since it is about a police detective investigating a murder, but it is also imbued with deep and—for Korea in the late 1970s—controversial ideas about the role of religion, particularly that of Protestant Christianity. Through the ruminations found in the journal of the murder victim and the slowly evolving consciousness of the detective who reads it, Yi presents an implicit but penetrating critique of blind or (perhaps more accurately) ignorant and uninformed faith. The murder mystery in *Son of Man* becomes ultimately secondary to what the reader learns about religion, and for a Korean public engaged with the volatile religious politics of the late 1970s, it was shocking and also disillusioning. Yi provides readers with an education on the evolution of Christianity, including a long discourse on Zoroastrianism, which made many of them reexamine the imported traditions of Christianity in a new light. For Western readers familiar with religion in Korea, his reinterpretation of the figure of Ahasuerus the Wandering Jew, whose curse resonates so much with Yi's own life, is especially fraught with political meaning.

Likewise, Yi's twist on the tradition of hagiography, *Hail to the Emperor*, presents a poignant allegory of Korean history, addressing its transition from the Joseon-era worldview to modernity through the epic tale of a deluded "emperor," the leader of a nationalist cult hidden in the mountains. *Hail to the Emperor* produces the effect one might achieve by applying the narrative structure of *The Great Gatsby* to convey the theme of illuminated madness in *King Lear*. In the surface narrative, set in the present, a jaded journalist is sent into the remote mountains to write an investigative human interest piece, but in the process of interviewing an old man—the surviving keeper of rituals for the strange cult—he becomes a convert, and to his own surprise he ends up writing a traditional-style hagiographical "history." Through this unusual structure, which appears to be a bracketed story missing its closing bracket, Yi provides a unique commentary on the dynamics of Korea's social, cultural, political, and religious transformations in the modern era.

Hail to the Emperor is often considered a difficult novel for contemporary readers. Its erudition is profound, and it exemplifies Yi's command of Korea's classical literature as it alludes to central texts in the Confucian, Taoist, and shamanic folk traditions, making reference to Chinese classics with the same ease as it portrays commonplace beliefs from indigenous folk religion.

Because of his deep engagement with tradition, even while he problematizes it, Korean critics have tended to label Yi as a conservative writer, and it is probably the influence of these critics that caused the current younger readership, with their progressive politics and demands for liberalization, to regard Yi as a conservative. Some academics are of the opinion that the new conservatism of the current Park administration (a legacy and reminder of Park Chung-hee's military dictatorship, as it is headed by his daughter) may create a resurgence in Yi's popularity because his work is constantly measuring the pulse of national sentiment. According to Lee Tao-dong, a prominent literary critic, "behind Korean literature's transition from the oppressed 1980s to the exploration of new horizons in the 1990s is the invisible hand of Yi Mun-yol" (Yi, 77).

But at a time when younger and more popular Korean writers are going out of their way to present themselves as "international" or "nationless" writers, Yi is probably the one Korean writer whose work is read most clearly from outside the constraints of Korean national and literary politics—precisely because his work represents Koreans in all of their political and psychological complexity. It is an irony befitting his novels that his own outsiderhood makes his work so resonant.

Shin Dong-uk, another prominent critic, classifies the characters in Yi's work as being socially and intellectually alienated men "driven by the desire for self-realization, which is inexorably linked to the ever-changing society" (Yi, 79). One sees the theme of outsiderhood play out to a significant degree in nearly all of Yi's works. Four of his novels provide particular insight into that condition: *Age of Heroes*, with a great deal of background about Yi's childhood, particularly the multigenerational stigma of his father's betrayal of the South; *Periphery*, which he wrote in response to criticism and which depicts the autobiographical main character as a maladjusted and deeply reflective outsider; *Everyone Who Falls Has Wings*, a confessional murder mystery that slowly becomes a psychological tour de force—an incisive depiction and indictment of the postcolonial Korean male psyche; and *The Poet*, one of his most important works, a historical novel that can be read as a kind of allegorical intellectual autobiography.

In the tradition of much Korean literature, *The Poet*, though fiction, is deeply rooted in personal experience, blending the notion of fiction and nonfiction in a way similar to the old histories, which merge historical fact, folklore, and mythology. One of the qualities that makes *The Poet* so resonant is that the story of its main character, based on the nineteenth-century historical figure Kim Byeong-yeon (better known as Kim Sakkat the "Rainhat" poet), seems to have its thematic parallels nearly tailored to Yi's own life. In a 2014 interview, Yi said:

> I started writing this book in my mid-forties, reflecting on my life up to then. I was able to tell in one volume all the disparately expressed aspects of my life in different novels. My family was subject to much suffering for the longest time as a result of my father's defection to North Korea. And because of a guilt-by-association system, we were restricted from being part of mainstream society. Consequently, the resulting fright led me to remain mute or compliant to the political circumstances of the early 1980s—that has been a big burden on me. At the same

time, as I got older and acquired a political consciousness, I began to ask myself what was the best position for me to take about that time period. *The Poet* was a book in which I tried to resolve all these issues. (Hye, n.p.)

In his literary work, and in his private life, Yi not only responds to themes directly relevant to himself; he is also profoundly aware of the contemporary predicament of Korea—currently ranked the sixth most "wired" nation on the planet according to Bloomberg—in the age of the Internet and media manipulation. It is not only the younger generation of Koreans that is ruled by consumerism, narcissism, and hunger for fame and fortune. Yi's work seems to be designed precisely to be disillusioning, and perhaps even traumatic, to such a readership because it dares to go against the grain of both popular and normative thinking. His novels cannot be engaged superficially for the sake of entertainment or distraction, nor do they take on the Murakami-esque tone of melancholic alienation regarded as a symptom of contemporary society and so popular with younger writers. In the current literary landscape of Korea, Yi may be seen as a throwback to older times, but actually he is a breath of fresh air—or perhaps more like a blast of cold air.

The critic Lee Nam-ho succinctly characterized Yi's writings as "an exceptionally useful guide for young intellectuals trying to attain a deeper understanding of the world than what they were taught in school, and to proactively encounter reality and the incongruities of the world" (Yi, 83). It is no surprise, then, that Yi is one of South Korea's repeat nominees for the Nobel Prize in Literature.

I met Yi Mun-yol for the first time in 2001, long before I began translating his work. I was on a panel to discuss the screening of the 1992 movie based on *Our Twisted Hero* (1987; English translation, 2001) at the New School's Tishman Auditorium in New York City. The film played to a packed audience, and it was in comparing the film adaptation to the text that I first began to appreciate Yi's unusual use of language, particularly his method of layering thematic and psychological qualities under what appeared, on the surface, to be a rather straightforward and expository style. While the film's director, Park Chong-won, had used overt symbolism, such as the image of an American silver dollar in flames to represent both the destruction of liberty and the power of the paper dollar in Korea, Yi had already charged the text with a range of allegorical resonances with simple touches like the use of character names that had multiple homophonic readings. Until that time, I had believed the general sentiment that Yi's writing tended to be expository, abstract, and political.

My second meeting with Yi Mun-yol happened while he was a fellow at Harvard University's Korea Institute in 2007. He was lecturing on Korean Literature along with David McCann, who was discussing *sijo* poetry. I was introduced to Yi by Lee Young-Jun, managing editor of *Azalea: Journal of Korean Literature & Culture*, published by Harvard's Korea Institute. Lee, who had been one of Korea's most important literary editors before coming to the United States for his PhD, told me that Yi was supposed to be studying English as part of his residency at Harvard but that, in his characteristic way, he tended to spend more time on impromptu teaching and lecturing. I don't know if Yi's command of the English language improved all that much during that year, but his residency at Harvard had a significant impact on the study of Korean literature in the United States.

Because of my own status as a writer and literary scholar, and because I had copyedited some of his other works that had been translated into English, Yi asked me for suggestions on how his work should best be translated. He regretted that his own English was not good enough for him to assess the literary quality of his novels in English, and he invited me to try my hand at translating some of his stories to re-create the layered effects he worked so hard to produce in Korean. His ideal model, he said, was the way Edward Seidensticker had worked with Kawabata Yasunari on *Snow Country*, and he generously offered to make himself available at any time to answer questions or even to make revisions for the sake of accessibility in English. Later that year, as I was editing the special North Korea section of the next issue of *Azalea*, which attracted a great deal of attention because Kim Jong-il was prominently in the news at the time, I asked Lee Young-Jun if Yi had written anything on North Korea. That is how I was first introduced to *Meeting with My Brother*.

I began translating *Meeting with My Brother* with Yoosup Chang, a former student of mine who provided valuable insight into contemporary colloquialisms and narrative tone, but while we were still in the middle of the novella, Lee Young-Jun approached me with the idea of translating one of Yi's controversial short stories. He recommended a story in which Yi exposes the hypocrisy of the Confucian preoccupation with patrilineage under the guise of a female schoolteacher's confessional memoir. This was "An Anonymous Island," which eventually appeared in the special 9/11 commemorative issue of the *New Yorker* in 2011—the magazine's first piece of fiction by a Korean writer.

After my own close reading of the Korean edition and reviewing responses to Suh Ji-moon's earlier translation, which she had called *An Appointment with My Brother* (2002), I pointed out to Yi that many of the matter-of-fact allusions to Korean history and culture would be opaque to American readers. In response, he added a few small glosses, and where there was a significant need for a concrete dramatic evocation of the Korean War narrative, he provided an additional scene that is absent in the original Korean edition and Suh's translation. It is the narrator's memory of his father's departure, a scene that many Korean readers might have been able to infer from their knowledge of Yi's past—an essential element of the story to be made vivid to the English readership.

Yi is meticulous about his use of Korean (down to the etymological roots of words), and he was interested in the idea of translation as a re-creation of associations in the target language. He was happy to see that I understood his use of character names in his novels as a kind of physiognomy; he glossed his own given name, Mun-yol—文烈—for me as "Literary Fire" and jokingly suggested I keep that in mind as a standard for the new translation. Yi understood the limitations of a lexically based translation and was open to the restructuring of sentences as often being a necessity to preserve the original sequence of images and associations. For me, this made the task of translating *Meeting with My Brother* less constrained but at the same time more challenging.

Meeting with My Brother is an unusual novella—at first glance it appears to be a rather journalistic version of the well-understood post–Korean War metaphor of separated brothers as divided nation, but it does not participate comfortably in this literary trope. Philip Gourevitch, writing in the *New Yorker* in 2003, noted, "There is no moral to Yi's story, only the awareness that this is what Korea has come to: half brothers, living in their respective half countries, who have inherited a situation that neither one wants and that weakens them both, and binds them by keeping them apart." In a world that seems to be terrified by the constantly escalating threats posed by the North Korean regime and yet is also curiously riveted by the most current antics of the hermit nation's idiosyncratic lineage of Kims, Yi Mun-yol's *Meeting with My Brother* offers a sobering, disillusioning, and yet poignant and hopeful perspective on the volatile relationship between the divided Koreas.

The novella, like many of Yi's works, is highly autobiographical. Yi told me that although his mother clung to the unrealistic hope that the family might someday be reunited, he himself had decided that his father was mostly likely dead once he heard that the elder Yi had been purged sometime in the mid-1950s. It wasn't until the mid-1980s that Yi's family received a letter from his father and learned that he had survived for thirty years in various prison camps and now had a new wife and five other children. It went without saying that his father would never return to the South, nor—given the laws of the time—was it possible to correspond with him. *Meeting with My Brother* is the product of Yi's decades of imagining his father's circumstances combined with the story of a fictional narrator's trip to Yanji, a Chinese city just north of the northern tip of North Korea, where it was possible to arrange for a meeting with someone smuggled across the border.

The plot of *Meeting with My Brother* is straightforward, and most of it parallels his own life. The fictionalized Yi, the main character and narrator, is a middle-aged South Korean university professor whose father had abandoned his family at the outbreak of the Korean War and defected to the North. Yi has lived with this stigma all his life, and when he learns that his father is still alive after more than forty years of no contact, he engages in a long and risky process of setting up a meeting in China. Unfortunately, his intermediary takes so long with the arrangements that his father passes away in the interim, and the novella opens with Professor Yi agreeing to meet with his younger half-brother instead.

As one might predict from such a situation, the meeting is initially charged with bitterness and recrimination, and since we come to the meeting ourselves with a Western bias, we tend to be on the side of Professor Yi. But what we learn from Yi's half-brother is a surprise. What Yi and the reader might want to dismiss, at first, as the product of North Korean brainwashing, is shocking for its matter-of-factness. It is not the story we would expect to hear from a man whose family did well for themselves in the most repressive regime on earth.

Yi maintains a veneer of anonymity to protect the identities of the central characters in *Meeting with My Brother*, since the novella includes politically charged conversations with the likes of "Mr. Reunification," "the businessman," and a madam who once tried to find work in the South. Although it was first published in Korea in 1994, nearly everything in it still has immediate relevance twenty-five years later. There is nothing else like it currently available in English—even in Korean there are no literary works that approach this theme with Yi's combination of a dispassionate political and economic perspective along with a poignant personal and cultural insight. *Meeting with My Brother* reads like it could be a piece of undercover investigative journalism, but it is also, importantly, an allegorical autobiography. An antidote, a counterpoint, and an expansion of everything we have come to associate with North Korea from Western media coverage, *Meeting with My Brother* is bound to be both controversial and illuminating for readers with an interest in the divided Koreas.

REFERENCES

Gourevitch, Philip. "Alone in the Dark." *The New Yorker*, August 8, 2003.

Hye Yisoo. "Tumultuous Era, Songs of Violent Passions: The World of Yi Mun-yol in His Own Words" (LTI Korea interview #1 with Yi Mun-yol). *_list Books from Korea* 26 (winter 2014).

Yi Mun-yol. *Pilon's Pig*. Trans. Jamie Chang. Seoul: Asia Publishers, 2013.

acknowledgments

Many thanks to Professors David McCann and Lee Young-Jun for introducing me to Yi Mun-yol and re-introducing me to his work; and thanks to Jennifer Crewe and Jonathan Fiedler of Columbia University Press for their support and patience through the process of publication. I am also grateful to Yi Mun-yol for his steadfast patience and support over the years. Special thanks to Yoosup Chang for lending his colloquial ear and to Bella and Anne for reading and providing feedback on early drafts of the translation.

meeting *with*
my brother

My brother did not show up. Not because of some unforeseen circumstance, but probably because we hadn't nailed down a specific date for the meeting. Mr. Kim explained why our plans kept falling through by stressing how it was his first time doing this sort of work. From the way his dark, gaunt face turned noticeably red and how he squirmed at certain points like a scolded child, this was probably true.

"They told me it was good money, and it seemed like a good deed, you know, arranging a meeting between a long-lost father and son," he said. "I took the job because everybody else is doing it. I didn't think it would be so hard, but I was so wrong! It looked like quick work, then it all fell apart. Just a lot of talk—going from this one to that one until it all ends up being nothing but hot air.

"I spread a lot of cash around in the most ridiculous places. By the time I found out where your father was, after digging all over North Korea, it was already two weeks after his funeral. But don't you worry this time. Your brother—he might be a day or two late, but he'll be here for sure."

It seemed that Mr. Kim had already told me everything he needed to, but he wouldn't leave. Little by little, I grew tired of him. Maybe he sensed this, because he stopped rehashing the same lines and started telling me stories about what he'd seen in North Korea—tragic stories I already knew, because he had already told me or I'd heard them elsewhere. He exaggerated a bit, mostly about the food shortage. Like most people from the border region of Yanbian, he gave out information to be friendly and to ingratiate himself. But it was really his wife who went into North Korea. When he touched on things I actually wanted to know about, all he had to offer was conjecture and hearsay—and I already had plenty of that myself.

Does he want the rest of the money? I thought when we had run out of things to say and were just sitting there looking at each other. It might seem cold of me, but after two failures, I had no intention of paying him the remainder of his fee—not quite half—before the job was done. I'd often been warned to be careful because the Korean Chinese were tired and jaded these days, but it was his lack of decisiveness and not so much his integrity that I distrusted.

But the matter of money was my own hasty conclusion. As I sat there silently, not having the heart to tell him to leave, he hesitated, then said suddenly, "I know this isn't your first time here, but have you seen all of Yanji? If you haven't, I'd like to . . . uh . . . show you around."

I finally realized he'd been lingering because he felt guilty for not having done his job, and now I appreciated the kindness. But I didn't really welcome his suggestion. I'd already spent an entire day touring the area around Yanji back in the late eighties, following the Hairan River, looking for Yongdurae, the Dragon Well . . . I'm not that interested in sightseeing anymore. I might feel a vague sense of the exotic the day I land in a new country, but by the next morning, everything is as unremarkable as it is at home. That's how traveling feels to me now.

I showed Mr. Kim out, making various polite excuses in an effort not to be rude. When I looked at the clock, it was already after eleven. He had spent nearly two hours telling me what he could have said in a simple sentence: "Your brother couldn't make it." I'd heard that Kim was employed by a state-run company, but if he could waste an entire morning on a workday, it must have been a pretty inefficient business.

I had been introduced to Mr. Kim by Professor Ryu of Yanji University, whom I'd met at an ancient history seminar that was actually just a pretext for visiting Mt. Baekdu, the volcano in North Korea where the mythic ancestor of the Korean people descended from Heaven. Then, as now, North and South Korea were strictly cut off from each other, and travel to and from China was very difficult. That kind of subterfuge was the only way to visit Heaven Lake on top of Mt. Baekdu.

You would get an entrance visa issued in China for the purpose of academic exchange, then go to Yanji and sit through a seminar, then squint at the lake from Mt. Changbai on the Chinese-controlled side of Mt. Baekdu. Professor Ryu presented his research on the Northeast region, focusing on the history of Pohai, but I didn't befriend him because of his scholarly expertise. I just happened to like his simple and modest character.

Two days before I left for the port of Yantai—which was how I returned to South Korea by boat at the end of my earlier trip—I mentioned that I wanted to see the Tumen River, and Professor Ryu graciously became my guide. Together we headed to Changbai, a town on the Chinese side of the Tumen across from the North Korean city of Hyesan. Because we were upstream, the Tumen wasn't very wide there, and as we looked over at North Korean soil my thoughts naturally turned to my father, a naïve revolutionary who chose the North as his homeland when he left the South in the middle of the brutal war. I thought of him abandoning his young wife and three kids in hell so he could seek his own nation by himself—he was approaching eighty now, living out the rest of his days in that gloomy landscape—and I suddenly needed a drink.

Could I have had a premonition as I left the hotel? I had an unopened bottle of the local wine and a handful of jerky in my bag. I took them out—ignoring Professor Ryu's polite refusals—and with a catch in my voice, I started to tell him the story of my young father, nearly twenty years younger than I am now, his poor wife and children, his wasting away in obscurity in the North for the remainder of his life. I slowly got drunk without realizing it, and started weeping and acting like a fool, pouring a drink onto the ground and making a ceremonial bow toward North Korea. My father was still alive at that time—I had performed a mockery of a Confucian memorial service—but Professor Ryu only watched in silence and waited for my emotions to cool.

"Why don't you try hiring someone, Professor Yi?" he asked. "Have someone here make the arrangements. It should be possible for you to set up a meeting with your father."

Of course, I had heard of such things. I had made time I didn't really have to attend that pretense of a seminar because, in my heart, I was looking for exactly that—a meeting. But I had been intimidated by a stern warning from the Security Planning Board, the South Korean counterpart of the CIA. I was concerned about my status as a professor at a national university, and so I had met with an SPB agent through a connection. But before I could even mention my concern, he'd cut me short with a lecture.

"Look, Professor," he said. "In the current situation where a Korean-Chinese diplomatic treaty has yet to be signed, you could say that Yanji is semi–North Korean territory. Even if our agents were to follow you, there is no way we could guarantee your safety for a secretive meeting like that. Frankly, if a few North Korean Special Service agents tailed your father and whisked you off to North Korea, that would make you a hero up there. They'd say you defected. Do you think you'd ever be able to claim it was really a kidnapping? What would be the use, anyway?

"So forget about making contact with your father in Yanji at this time. It's still too early. If you were just an ordinary citizen, I wouldn't bother to warn you like this. But you're a professor at a leading national university and a nationally prominent scholar. You've got enemies on many different fronts.

"I'm asking you not to try this because . . . if it goes badly, it wouldn't just be unfortunate for you and your family. It would have national repercussions. Of course, we can appreciate the urgency you feel with your father being nearly eighty. It's only natural that a son would want to see his father, even just once, before he passes away. But you can't rush into this. We'll keep you in mind, Professor. We'll do our best to work out some different venue. So please, this time, just attend that seminar and come right back."

I could hardly arrange a secret meeting after that, so I wasted five days on a boring seminar and a lackluster tour of Mt. Baekdu, which I had already seen in pictures. No wonder my emotions had finally come to a head.

I accepted Professor's Ryu's suggestion—feeling like I was entering into some criminal conspiracy—and he sent Mr. Kim to my hotel the next day. Kim's wife was a North Korean national living legally in China, and her family was still in North Korea, in Cheongjin. She also had three uncles scattered in Pyongyang, Uiju, and Hoeryeong, respectively. That was why I thought of giving Mr. Kim the job—the fact that he had connections in Cheongjin and Pyongyang. My father's letter from the mid-eighties had a Pyongyang address, and more recently, a relative from Japan who came to see me had told me he'd met my father in Cheongjin.

I wrote out a list for Mr. Kim containing every bit of personal information I remembered about my father. I gave him an advance of three thousand dollars—borrowing from my colleagues what they could spare—and had him make the arrangements for me to meet my father in Yanji. It was an unusual contract. I guaranteed him twenty thousand yuan on top of his actual fee, and promised that I would take care of any additional expenses due to my father's special status. I also had a personal guarantee from Professor Ryu.

It must have been a lot of money for Mr. Kim, because he came with his wife to see me the morning I left Yanji. He was full of excitement and painted a rosy picture. He would be able to arrange a meeting as early as winter break that year—only a couple of months away—or by the following spring at the latest. He was optimistic, he said, because even in North Korea the middle leadership class was thoroughly corrupt and there wasn't much that couldn't be bought with the almighty dollar.

But progress was slow. I didn't have high expectations, but that winter break went by without any news, and then summer came and still there was no news.

Since I was doing something illegal at the time, I couldn't exactly write to Mr. Kim or send someone to nag him. I spent a year waiting impatiently. Then Korea and China established diplomatic relations and my frustration was amplified, because now the risk the SPB had warned me about was gone.

Finally, in January, Professor Ryu came to Seoul to visit a relative, and he brought unexpected news.

"I'm sorry," he told me. "It turns out your father passed away last summer. Would you believe Kim Hanjo, that idiot, knew about it, but only told me just now? It seems his wife was sick in bed for a few months, but even so, he must have thought his dawdling had fouled things up and he was too ashamed to face you. He spent the rest of your money going in and out of North Korea, still trying to arrange something even after that. . . ."

Then Professor Ryu casually made a new suggestion. I don't know whether it was on behalf of Mr. Kim, or his own idea. "Kim is worried sick because he knows he has to pay you back, but do you think it can be done? Three thousand dollars . . . In Yanji you'd need to sell your house to get that kind of money. So, I was thinking . . . your father is already gone, but how would you like to meet a brother of yours instead? It seems you have a couple over there."

I honestly did not even hear what Ryu was suggesting. All the love and hate, all the longing and resentment, pent up inside me for half a century suddenly went up in smoke, leaving me entirely empty. My emotions were no longer as violent as when I was young, but still—the object of my longing and hatred, who still appeared to me constantly in different guises, leaving this world so pathetically . . .

I had been anxious to meet my father because he was getting old—approaching eighty—and yet the sudden news of his death made it seem unreal and absurd. My last memory of him was as a young man still in his mid-thirties.

After leaving Professor Ryu without making any sort of commitment, all I could think of on my way home was my father's death. Should I tell my mother? What traditional funerary ceremonies should I perform in this situation? There were so many pressing decisions I had to make.

In the late eighties, when my mother learned that my father had sired five children with his second wife in the North, she

never mentioned him again, not even once. To my mother—
who was beyond the slightest reproach, raising three children
on her own and staying faithful to my father all those years—
this evidence of his fertility amounted to a great betrayal.
What would news of his death mean to her now?

As the eldest son, I was responsible for carrying out the traditional Confucian funerary rituals. My father had already
been dead for some time, but I wondered if I still had to find
a funeral home and put on traditional mourning clothes. How
would I end the period of mourning? Would it be acceptable
for me to hold the annual memorial rite in the North, or would
we need to hold a separate ritual through a temple or church
for transferring his remains? What about the family registry
in the South that shows Father as still living? If I filed a
notification of his death, would it be accepted? Should I
notify the clan about Father's death when they're in the middle
of rewriting their genealogy, or should I wait until I can have
my five siblings in the North added to the record?

In the end, there wasn't much I could do. Whom would I
notify, and what sort of ritual was appropriate when all we
had was secondhand news—not much more than a rumor,
really—of his death? And I didn't know the circumstances or
even the exact date of his passing. I wondered if it might be
all right to tell my mother, but even that didn't seem proper.
She had begun to show unmistakable signs of senility that
winter, and I had no way of knowing how the shock would
affect her.

First, I had to get all the facts. When I had finally organized my thoughts, I felt I had a reason to meet my brother
from the North. Until then, I had only listened half-heartedly

to news about him, as if it had nothing to do with me. He was just an obscure figure I imagined I would meet someday after reunification, but now—because he had a specific connection to my life—he had actually begun to exist.

When Professor Ryu was about to return home, I sent word to him that I had decided on the meeting, and this time Mr. Kim made rapid progress, as if to make up for his previous failure. I got news from Yanji in less than two months. On the surface, it was just a note, an ordinary letter written in Korean, but it contained a date in the code we had agreed upon: *Today*.

It was mid-semester. I hurried to get ready for my trip. Diplomatic relations had been formalized between Korea and China, but it was still hard to get a visa for that kind of personal trip because South Korean security was as strict as ever. It was risky. If the relationship between the countries became hostile again, I could be arrested under the National Security Law for illegally crossing the border and having a clandestine meeting.

I thought about it carefully and decided on a seven-night Mt. Baekdu tour with Yanji as the halfway point. I left Seoul, tagging along with a group from a travel agency whose schedule suited me.

E ven as I was practically pushing Mr. Kim out the door, I realized that I wanted to be rid of his solicitude, especially his boring repetition of trivial things. But once I was alone, I had a sudden and urgent need to rest. It had taken several days to get to Yanji and I was tired from the tour of China, which had never interested me in the first place, but I think what

really drained me was the anxiety building up in me as I anticipated meeting with my brother.

I'm meeting my younger brother for the first time in my
life, I thought. I don't even know his face. A half-brother. A
brother who's reached middle age, who grew up and was educated in a completely different culture and environment for
close to forty years. I set out for Yanji with a detailed and
emotional scenario in my mind, but as the time of the meeting
approached, my nervousness made the scenario less and less
plausible. I slept fitfully, waking in the middle of the night,
trying to restage that shaky scene in my head. The next
morning the screen would be blank again—at least on the
surface. But I must have been anxious and exhausted under-
neath. When I heard that my brother still hadn't arrived, I
felt a strange relief and a desire to get some rest.

I drew the curtains and lay down, intending to have a good
nap. I had plenty of time since Professor Ryu was supposed
to come see me at three. He had called early that morning to
apologize for not being able to rush over—he had organized
some event for a group from Korea that had arrived a few
days earlier.

But I couldn't sleep for long. I lay in bed dozing fitfully.
When some insignificant noise woke me, I could not get back
to sleep no matter how hard I tried. When I thought about
how expensive this trip was, I felt guilty about sleeping in
my hotel room in the middle of the day.

Finally, I went downstairs for some coffee. The hotel café
was busier than any we'd seen in other cities. Since this hotel
was where Korean travelers stayed, the café looked like a
meeting place for the locals and South Koreans. I found an

empty seat and ordered a coffee, but before it arrived, a man who was just getting up after meeting with someone waved and came over to me.

"I didn't realize you stayed behind, too, Professor! I guess you've seen Heaven Lake before? These days you'd have to be a real hick not to have seen it."

I watched as he sat down across from me without even asking. He was someone I'd spent the past few days with, a member of my tour group. I'd noticed him for his friendly manner, but also because he talked too much.

"Oh, yes," I said. "I saw it last spring."

"Then you must be here on business. They say it's easy to get an individual visa if it's for business. So why did you join the tour?"

I was taken aback for a moment because I hadn't told him I was an academic. But he must have guessed. I decided to play along.

"No special reason," I said. "I figured I'd see the sights for a day or two and take care of some business while I'm here. What about you?"

I was evasive because I didn't want to reveal the purpose of my trip. I wasn't actually interested in why he'd stayed behind, but I got the sense that he didn't want me to find out .

"Same here," he said. "I do have a business, but it's not something I can talk about openly. There's no direct flight from Seoul to Yanji, you know, . . . and I've never been to Guilin or Xi'an, either . . . part of the itinerary."

For a chatterbox, he was oddly cautious, and if he was trying to be evasive, he wasn't very good at it. That quietly piqued my curiosity. So why *had* he stayed behind?

Before I could ask him another question, he abruptly changed the subject. "Come to think of it," he said, "three of us stayed behind. I thought it was just me and Mr. Reunification."

I already knew about Mr. Reunification. He was an activist—notorious from the start for being a different kind of chatterbox than this mystery man—and he had suggested the nickname himself. He had a passionate interest in the lost glories of ancient Korea, and whenever he could get anyone's attention he tried very hard to educate them about the subject.

When he landed in Beijing his first words were, "This land belonged to Baekje. When Baekje ruled over Yoseo and Jinpyeong, Beijing was a part of Jinpyeong. In fact, the whole of central China was ours until the Han people crowded in." He spouted similar things at the Forbidden City: "Yi Seong-gye, the founder of the Joseon Dynasty, should have kept advancing into China. Then the Forbidden City would have been ours! You think the Manchus were so great? I mean, the first Manchu emperor, Nurhahi, conquered the Ming with just thirty thousand men from his eight cavalry divisions. But two hundred years before that, Yi Seong-gye lost his nerve and turned back at Wi Hwa Do with an army of fifty thousand."

I imagine he was steeped in texts like *The Ancient Records of Hwandan* and *Bi Ryu's Chronicle of Baekje* that claim the ancient ancestors of the Koreans once ruled a large part of Northeast Asia. He got the nickname "Mr. Reunification" because—after enlightening us on all the glories of ancient Korea—he would always end by haranguing us about the importance of reunification. His rants grew more vehement once we got to Yanji.

"Look at this landscape! Isn't it just like Korea? And it's not because there are so many Koreans here. It's because the shapes of the mountains and rivers are totally unlike the rest of China! You could say we were in Gyeongsang or Chungcheong Province in southern Korea, and no one would know the difference.

"The Japs committed endless crimes. As if swallowing up our whole peninsula wasn't enough, they had to give away the contested Gando region to the Chinese! If only all the people who got displaced had settled in little by little and bided their time until they got vested rights, this would have been our land for sure!"

He had carried on like this on the bus ride from the airport to downtown Yanji, and last night he suddenly made an announcement at the dinner table, as if he were some important political exile.

"I'm not interested in seeing Mt. Baekdu. I'll be happy to see Heaven Lake after reunification—it will still be there. I'm spending those two days with local Koreans who know about the situation in North Korea. I want to see what I can do to further the cause of reunification."

To the others he must have appeared ridiculous, just a naïve amateur historian, but I saw him differently. He was more than that. Naïveté like his is a curious thing. People like him are usually seen as fools or comical dimwits, but sometimes what they do can be mistaken for dedication and their passion can evoke great emotion. Now and then my university invites well-known speakers to give talks on reunification, and half the time there is no difference between their naïveté and that of their undergraduate audiences. If Mr. Reunification had delivered his rant at a college festival hosted by a nationalistic student organization—and not to a tour group full of jaded and faded forty- and fifty-somethings—he might have convinced quite a few people. So I figured he was quite a formidable expert in such matters and had his own agenda from the start.

In fact, Mr. Reunification was the reason I had gone so far as to pay for a single room during our visit to Yanji. Otherwise, I would have had to share a double with him. I didn't want him to know why I was staying behind, and I didn't want to be around to witness his unwitting violation of the South Korean national security laws. Since what I was doing was also illegal, there was a strong possibility that we might implicate each other, which would have had terrible consequences. But the businessman who had also stayed behind in Yanji ended up sharing a room with Mr. Reunification.

"I'd have asked them to put me in a room with you if I'd known you were staying too, Professor. That reunification is noisy work," he said, making a face.

Hearing about it from an objective distance, I suddenly became interested in Mr. Reunification's work. Reunification was an idea I found hard to fathom, so I was curious to hear about someone for whom it was not just a vague possibility but an immediate necessity, someone with a clear idea of the methods, the particular steps that needed to be taken.

"What exactly is he doing with this reunification business?" I asked.

"It's all talk," said the businessman. "Just talk. Two groups came through this morning and you couldn't ask for a more serious-looking political rally. It was like they were ready to write one of those declarations in their own blood. What did they say . . . something like, 'Let's take to heart the heat of our common blood, the precious shared heritage of our people, and leap over the walls of ideology!' "

"What sort of people were they?"

"Professors, writers—they seemed to be pretty well-known around here. It was their first meeting with our Mr. Reunification, but they'd met a couple of times with other people from some group he's involved with. . . . The funny thing is, Mr. Reunification was getting all worked up, like he was talking to representatives of some government in exile. Saying things you might hear on North Korean broadcasts. 'Let's destroy colonialism and achieve the people's independence! Let's wipe out the pro-Jap pro-Yankee traitors and advance our reunification!' Now I'm terrified I might get called in and interrogated by the Security Agency when I get home—just for the crime of having shared a room with him for a few days."

I didn't know what he did for a living, but this businessman was a good talker. Trying hard not to be obvious, I egged him on to hear more of his story. "I suppose there's a need for that kind of work for reunification to happen," I said. "Especially given what the U.S. has been up to since the Soviet Union collapsed."

"Nah, it's hopeless. I could tell from just looking at their faces. I don't think those people were actually interested in reunification at all. I think they were more interested in making a connection with a South Korean so they could start a joint business venture here or get invited to the South. But Mr. Reunification has no sense and just keeps talking, so they're reluctantly going along with it. What the hell is he thinking, anyway?"

"What do you mean?"

"He was making promises this morning. He said he'd get invitations for two people and that he'd donate several thousand books to some group. And he was bragging about a school somewhere, promising to get some millionaire to build them a library. He doesn't seem to have that kind of pull, in my opinion. He might be setting up the simple people here for disappointment."

If he was badmouthing Mr. Reunification to distract me from asking about his own business, he wasn't doing a very good job of it. As he kept talking, the conversation started to circle back around to him.

"People are really strange," he said. "Why is it when they talk about reunification, they only think about ideology and race? Is it like that for you, too, Professor?"

As careful as I had been to hide the fact, he must have sensed I was an academic because he insisted on calling me "Professor" even though I had told him that I, too, was a businessman. "Well," I said, "what comes to mind when *you* think of reunification?"

"How to feed those twenty million starving people—not counting Pyongyang citizens. How much money it will take to give North Korea a paint job so it looks like the South, at least on the surface?"

"The big companies must be able to come up with something," I said. "Once reunification happens, we'd get a lot of cheap labor, and we won't have to import expensive raw materials from far away. . . ."

"You don't know what you're talking about! One of my clients runs a major company, and he's really worried about the North Korean workers we'd have to support after reunification. The guest workers we use from Bangladesh, Pakistan, and the Philippines are dirt cheap, but he wonders if we could exploit our fellow Koreans like that. How would we deal with the new regional conflict that would produce? All the old problems we have between the southern provinces like Yeongnam and Honam would pale by comparison.

"He said the quality of North Korean labor was also bound to be a problem. There would be the typical inefficiency of socialist countries, but they'd also have the old fashioned idea of 'doing it our way'—which just won't fly for a modern workforce. He said if they're only good for manual labor in basic industries, they'd just be a liability.

"He's not very optimistic about North Korea's natural resources, either. They may have more than the South, but those that meet international standards—you could count them on your fingers. We could get trapped—buying all our raw materials from the North, even if they're more expensive and lower quality, just because they're from our own land. To be blunt, North Korean raw materials are more likely than not to be a burden on our industry."

"But couldn't that just be considered part of the cost of reunification?" I asked. "We're calculating how much it would cost and getting ready for it. Don't you think there'll be some solution—I mean economically? But I also think we need to get ready politically, like our Mr. Reunification says. If the country gets back together before things are sorted out ideologically, we may be in for another bloody war."

"I have a friend who sees it like this," said the businessman. "He says the most likely time for a communist revolution would be around three to five years after reunification. He says the standard of living in South Korea would go down because of the economic burden. There would be more poverty. The North Koreans would be even more impoverished. That means the malcontents would outnumber those who want to maintain the political status quo—and that ratio would make the population more susceptible to communism.

"Anyway, I'm just a salesman, so to me economic preparation seems more urgent. You saw the fall of the Soviet Union—ideology follows the economy, right? Those guys said the superstructure is built on the infrastructure."

When he called himself a salesman again, it awakened the curiosity I'd suppressed. The more he talked, the more I began to suspect he wasn't your everyday salesman.

"You said one of your clients ran a major company," I said. "I'm hearing a lot of things from you that most people don't seem to know. What sort of sales are you in?" I knew he was trying hard to avoid the issue, but I asked him again.

A look of uneasiness crossed his face, and he said, still evasively, "Oh, it's nothing much. This and that—whatever makes money . . ."

Then, spotting someone who'd just walked into the coffee shop with a large plastic bag, he leaped up from his seat and waved like a man signaling to a rescuer.

When I first came to Yanji in 1988—the year of the Seoul Olympics—the city had the distinct appearance of a socialist country. It felt like you were looking at an old electronic appliance—modern hardware with no software to run it. When I returned in 1992, four years later, a great deal had changed. The city's outward appearance wasn't that different, but the interior had been transformed to such a degree that I wondered if I was actually in Yanji. For better or worse, this change was caused by a move toward a market economy.

Another year-and-a-half had passed since then. . . . I headed toward Friendship Avenue to see what was different, as if I were conducting a formal inspection. I'd heard that this street had undergone the most radical changes, even for Yanji, but there were also lots of Korean restaurants there, so I thought I'd take a walk and find a place to have lunch. But the transformation of a city can be hard to perceive. Perhaps the changes would be too subtle to stimulate senses dulled by a half century of living? I strolled around just for the sake of walking—the streets seemed the same and yet different after two years, and it became physically taxing before I got very far. That's how I ended up at a place called the "Han River." The sign was in large Korean letters under a semicircle of English that read, "Café & Restaurant," probably for the benefit of South Korean tourists. It was a style I'd often seen in Seoul, and it gave me a familiar feeling.

Inside, even the décor seemed to have been transplanted from a cheap Seoul café. There were no customers. It wasn't quite lunchtime yet, and judging from the slow business, it looked like the place was more café than restaurant. I wasn't really planning on eating there.

"Come in," a woman's voice called from the shadows behind the counter. I couldn't be sure from her short greeting, but she didn't seem to have the local Yanji accent. She came over to me as I found an empty table. She appeared to be around thirty.

"What would you like?"

When she handed me a menu and asked again what I'd like, her accent sounded so much like the Seoul dialect that I did a double take. She was dressed the way a proprietor of a café in Seoul would dress, and for a moment I wondered if she was from there, but then decided against it. I'd heard that people from the South were starting lots of businesses here in Yanji, but why bother opening a second-rate café? I couldn't imagine a woman from Seoul coming all the way to Yanji to be a hostess.

"I'll just have a glass of juice," I said. I was curious about her, so I tried a ploy I used when I wanted to chat with proprietresses of country cafés in the South. "Bring one for yourself, too, if you like."

The woman returned with two glasses of juice—she was obviously used to this sort of thing—and sat down with me. She might have been bored, since there were no other customers, or else her lack of self-consciousness meant she wasn't a local.

She spoke first. "You're not from around here," she said with exaggerated interest. "Where did you come from?"

I suppressed my curiosity about her for the moment. "I'm from Seoul," I said.

"Are you here alone?"

"No, I'm with a group. But I broke away to take care of some business."

"Are you a businessman?"

"Not really, I'm just meeting someone."

"Where's the rest of your group?"

"It's just a tour group. They're at Heaven Lake."

"When do they get back?"

I figured there was no reason to hide anything from her, so I told her the truth. "Tomorrow night. We're supposed to stay in the hotel together."

"Then bring them here tomorrow night," she said with a knowing look. "I'll take good care of you all. It may not be much, but we have karaoke here. And a lot of irresistibly beautiful girls, real killers."

"I'll tell them," I said. I had finally found an opening, so I asked her, casually, "Are you from here?"

She answered without much hesitation. "Yes. Not exactly Yanji, but I grew up nearby. Why? Don't I look like a local?"

"You don't sound like it. Have you ever been to Seoul?"

"Oh, my accent! Yes, I lived in Seoul for about two years. I got funny looks and there were a lot of other disadvantages, too, when people heard my accent so . . . I worked hard on a Seoul accent. Does it sound pretty close?"

"What do you mean by disadvantages of having a Yanji accent?"

"Once they find out you're from Yanji, they look down on you and try to cheat you. And when I had a job they'd try to grope me while I was working."

She must have gone to Seoul to make some money. I was curious about how she had managed to stay in Seoul for two years, what she had done during that time, but I'd already heard a lot about the hardships of Chinese Koreans and decided not to pursue it. The conversation stalled.

"So, how's business?" I asked after a lengthy pause.

The woman sipped her juice and let out a long sigh. "While I was in Seoul, I thought I could make piles of money if I opened a place like this up here. But it's hard. The locals can't afford the drinks and we're stuck having to wait around for tourists. So how busy could we be? At this rate, it looks like we'll blow all the money my husband and I saved over those two years of working our fingers to the bone doing unspeakable things."

She glanced toward the kitchen as she spoke. A man who looked prematurely aged, probably her husband, was watching us unhappily from the doorway. When I saw his tired and worn face, I could imagine their life in Seoul—him working like hell every day, even Sundays, and her working every tough odd job just to earn an extra cent.

I remembered what the "salesman" had said in the hotel coffee shop about North Korean workers after reunification, and it occurred to me that what happened to this couple might show what was in store for them. "What about money?" I asked. "Did they pay you a decent wages?"

The question must have taken her by surprise. The woman blinked, and when she understood, she pressed her lips together. "Decent wages?" she said. "As soon as they found out we were from Yanji, they'd try to lowball us. The only jobs that pay decently are the dirty and dangerous ones that no South Korean will do. I don't think my husband ever got his full paycheck—even when he was doing dangerous construction work. He says they always found some way to skim something off the top."

"But weren't you paid close to what the other Koreans were getting? I heard that workers from the Philippines or Bangladesh don't even get a third of what South Koreans make."

A blue flame seemed to flash in her eyes. "How can you compare them to us? We're one people who share the same blood, no matter how long we've been apart. . . ."

She lowered her voice and sneaked a quick glance toward the kitchen. "You're from Seoul, so I'm sure you've heard," she said quickly, "but do you know how I scrounged to make that money? I made it washing bloody underwear for prostitutes and getting groped by drunkards while I was bussing tables at a hostess club. What else but money would make a married woman put up with that sort of thing? I'm among the well educated here, but decent jobs are nowhere to be found. When I tried to work at a factory in the South, they said they'd pay me the same as a Filipino. Can you believe that? Why should I have to take that kind of treatment? I'm not lazy like them, and I understand Korean. How could they treat a fellow Korean like that . . . ?"

Her lips drew tight in a look of fresh resentment. I had just seen a living example of the problem the businessman had described so casually to me not an hour ago. I felt guilty about reopening old wounds and tried to be consoling.

"It must have been terrible," I said. "Koreans . . . they should know better."

"Seoul might be all right for making money for a few years, but you couldn't pay me enough to live there a minute longer." Making that declaration seemed to calm her down, and she added, politely, "Of course, I'm not saying all South Koreans are bad. There are some people I'm grateful to and many were kind to me."

I'd stayed too long for just a glass of juice, and the conversation had run out. But I was embarrassed about getting up to leave.

"This is a restaurant," I said. "I feel bad about going after only a glass of juice. But I've come through Guilin and Xi'an and haven't had a proper Korean meal for days. . . . I'd like to have some Korean food."

Once I was frank with her, she didn't pressure me to stay. "It's all right," she said. "We put up that sign, but we aren't equipped to serve much food. What we do have is mainly Western food. What did you have in mind, anyway?"

"I was hoping for some spicy soup and a bit of kimchi. That would be enough."

"Then I'll recommend a good place. If you go down this street a ways, there's a place called Seoul Restaurant. Try there. It's not just the name—they say the head chef studied in Seoul, so the food should suit a Seoul palate."

Thanks to her recommendation, I was able to leave the café without further guilt and have a Korean lunch, which I had been craving for days. The spicy beef soup and kimchi at the Seoul Restaurant were full of MSG and sugar—probably to cater to tourists—but it was good enough since I'd only had greasy Chinese food since we'd left Beijing.

Later I heard some things that would have made the businessman proud if he'd known. They confirmed exactly what he had told me.

Professor Ryu came to see me at the hotel around 3:00 p.m. as we had arranged. "Professor Yi, I just can't understand South Koreans," he said, puzzled and frustrated. "I've met a fair number of them, and I've even been to Seoul, but . . ."

"Why, what happened?"

"This isn't the first time—it's happened before. I just don't understand them. I work hard to arrange a North-South cultural exchange at their request, and then when it's nearly all set they embarrass me with ridiculous demands. This time, a group from the South called the Association of Writers for Reunification said they wanted to meet North Korean literary people, so my colleague Professor Chang did his best to set up some connections on the Northern end. I helped a little on the side, and we were halfway there.

"We thought hard about who to pick from the North. I tried to introduce the South Koreans to people who were a bit more open-minded and less political, since they themselves seemed to have a bit of a—how should I put it?—*radical* slant. Do you know what they said? They said the North Korean writers should be major, if not famous, literary figures, with at least a few nationally decorated writers included. So I told them those people are political cronies, not writers, and they wouldn't hear anything but propaganda and *Juche* self-reliance ideology from them. And they told me that's exactly the kind of people they want to meet!

"I understand that they would want to meet representative literary figures, but as I listened, I could see it wasn't their only aim. Actually, they had more in common with those Party cronies because of their own communist sympathies! I was speechless when they showed their true colors. They were all excited over Kim Il Sung myths, and they'd gone out of their way to collect all sorts of statistics on North Korea's superiority—stuff that's even discredited up here these days. They were more rabid than a two-bit North Korean academic. They'd fit right in with the officially decorated North Korean writers.

"But what kind of cultural exchange would that make for? How could a meeting like that be a North-South literary conference? It sounds more like a conspiracy or a political rally for *Juche* literature.

"The conservative writers from the South weren't much better. They're the ones who really need to meet the major literary figures, but what they want instead is a young star talking about 'openness' or some no-name writer who writes popular romances. So they're doing just the same thing—another conspiracy or political rally, meeting with people who already have the same views.

"What's the point of a cultural exchange, anyway? Isn't it to understand the differences and find commonalities between the North and South to prepare for the coming reunification? To think they call that cultural exchange— birds of a feather telling each other what they already think. Is that what passes for philosophy in a democratic society? I was so angry I left Professor Chang to suffer there with them and just got up and left."

So that was how a politicized "cultural exchange" could turn out—foreshadowing the disaster that might come of a reunification tainted by politics.

"You don't get full from the first bite, but I suppose that's how you have to begin, isn't it?" I said. "Could you expect anything more than conflict when you put two different cultures together?" I tried to soothe Professor Ryu, but my heart began to grow heavy, weighed down by the concern that the brother whom I would soon meet was from precisely that different culture.

The phone call from Mr. Kim late that night made my heart even heavier.

"He's here. Your younger brother. He got in just before dark. He says he'll stay at his maternal uncle's place tonight and come meet you at the hotel in the morning. See? What did I tell you? Didn't I say he might be a day or two late, but he'd definitely come?"

Kim's voice was excited, as if he were delivering news of a great victory, but for me the news was hardly good. I already knew my brother had asked his uncle in Yanji to invite him so he could leave North Korea to meet me. The fact that he had come all the way to Yanji and then gone straight to his uncle's house showed that he wasn't all that eager to see me. I couldn't get rid of that shadow in a corner of my heart.

But the feeling didn't last long. My brother was here. When I realized I would see him after one more night's sleep, the darkness in my heart began to lift with excitement and anticipation. *When morning comes, I will finally meet my brother whose face I have never seen, who is one of the closest blood ties I have in this world. What does he look like? How was he raised? What is he like? How did the children fare growing up with a father, unlike the three of us?*

In my overwrought mind a vivid memory suddenly ignited—of an early fall afternoon forty years ago—something I had completely forgotten. It was the day my father set out, never to return. I was nine years old.

The summer of 1950 felt thick and interminable to me. Seoul had been overrun by North Korean troops and it was oppressively heavy and hot under the pressure of war, but what made that summer so terribly long? Some say everyone was in a daze: the endless columns of People's Republic Army volunteers marching south, the straggling lines of United Nations POWs being dragged north, the horrific spectacle of public executions, the bombings that went on day after day and night after night. But to my nine-year-old self the ninety days of that summer felt as long and boring as a single tedious day. Perhaps it was because of school—we might as well have been on summer vacation from June 25th, the day the war began.

For several days the schoolyard was empty and the only people coming and going were those wearing red armbands. Children were able to go to school again beginning in early July through the efforts of the Socialist Women's Alliance and the People's Youth Alliance, but more than half the kids in every class stayed home because they had no teachers, making it feel like summer break. Classes were self-taught, or left to the propaganda departments. Trapped inside our classroom— hot and cramped, under the heavy tension of war—we grew agitated and squirmed in our seats after a few days of sneaking glances at each other while we played at self-instruction. Then there was the singing of grown-up songs like "The Red

Flag" and "The Song of General Kim Il Sung"—we had no idea what they meant, and that got boring after a few weeks.

Then, in late July, the real summer break began, longer and more boring than any other I remember. As the front—which had been pushing relentlessly south with every communist victory—came to a stalemate at the Nakdong River, the anxiety and urgency of the North Koreans was palpable even to us children. There was no more of the generosity and kindness they had shown to us during the early occupation of Seoul, and the bloodshot eyes of the school staff and Party workers began to reveal their paranoia and resentment. We no longer played in the streets—scared for reasons we didn't understand—and we could no longer go out into the hills and fields, so close to the center of the city in those days, because of unexploded mines and bombs. That summer vacation felt like a punishment, with tedium and boredom used to whip us. We missed our games, playmates, and playgrounds so much that we actually began to look forward to the first day of school in early September.

But in mid-September, from far off in the direction of the West Gate, came a sound ominous to my young ears. It was a sign. People gathered in secret to gossip and whisper after they heard the faint rumbling of what sounded like cannons or aerial bombing.

It wasn't as loud or immediate as the noise from the 25th to the 28th of June, when communist soldiers had finally come pouring into Seoul, but even I could sense a certain mood of urgency in the air. But when I asked the grown-ups, they all said they couldn't hear a thing. Even the occasional person who admitted to hearing the sound explained it away as the usual noise of war.

It was only my father—who attended the People's Council of Seoul—who winced at my question and answered me with a solemn look. "Some southern National Defense troops might be left there," he said. "There's nothing to worry about. Our brave People's Army will destroy them soon."

But the fateful day when I would see my father for the last time came less than a week later. It is still vivid in my mind. I had come home early because school was let out on some pretext. Father came running into the house, pale and stern looking as I had never seen him before. Outside the gate I could hear the impatient sound of an engine revving, waiting for him.

"Honey," he called. "My rucksack! Give me my rucksack! Quickly!"

My mother struggled to drag out a heavy rucksack, fully packed, and her eyes were filled with tears. When I saw her I knew what was happening, even with the unsophisticated consciousness of a nine-year-old: Father had to go on a long journey, and Mother had known this already—she had been preparing. My eyes burned with tears. Perhaps it was just from seeing my mother crying, but what I recall—quite clearly— is the sudden and indescribable sadness I felt at that moment as Father and Mother parted.

Perhaps my young soul was touched by the possibility that I would never, in my life, see him again. I whimpered, "Father, where are you g-g—? Where are you going?"

My sister, who was three years older, followed Mother out from the bedroom and asked the same question, looking at Father with her eyes full of tears. I think our family might have been unconsciously preparing for that final farewell.

Father must have sensed something ominous, too. He mimed shooting a gun and said with an awkward smile, "Father's going to go *bang*!" Still smiling awkwardly, he looked at me and my sister. I got the feeling he was trying to put us at ease by being funny.

But Mother was shocked. "What?" she said. "Are you saying you're going to fight? With a *gun*?"

Father glanced at her again, looking embarrassed. He must have realized it was too late to make jokes, and said, somberly, "I didn't tell you because I didn't want you to be scared. It's been ten days already. Hundreds of thousands of Yankee troops landed at Inchon. The People's Army did its best to stop them, but I think it's over. The Yankee army will push into Seoul by tomorrow.

"In a few days, that huge army will cut the Korean peninsula in half, and then not even half of our People's Army that advanced south to the Nakdong River will be able to make it back. When that time comes, anyone who can pick up a gun will have to fight to defend our People's Democratic Republic."

"But not you!" cried Mother. "You're a fifth generation only son! You're a bookworm who studied abroad at Tokyo University. You shouldn't even think of fighting. How can you say you're picking up a gun? You wouldn't have dared if your mother was still alive." Mother approached Father, as if to grab his lapels. "Stay here and hide, like you did before," she said. "Hide until the People's Army regroups and counterattacks."

I do not understand the power of memory. These were things too difficult for a child to grasp, and yet I remember it all clearly, as if I'd just heard their conversation moments ago.

"Why are you behaving like this with the children watching?" said Father. "You didn't bat an eye when those damned pro-Japanese police dragged me away, so what's this sudden display of weakness? Don't disappoint me now." Father tried to stop mother with a look of profound disapproval, but she wouldn't back down.

"That was when the world was calm and we were making a living, even if we were just scraping by. We paid for that smart lawyer by selling off our land for a pittance. We even had enough money to grease the palm of the detective who was investigating you. But not now. We've been through three months of hell, killing and being killed by each other, and where you're going, I can't help like I did before. You can't leave like this." Mother actually grabbed Father's lapels at that point, but just then the horn sounded from outside.

Father gently removed Mother's hands and spoke to her softly, with warmth in his eyes. "When I said 'pick up a gun,' I was just assuming the worst. Even if I joined the army, what kind of soldier would I make at my age? But in times like these I don't think I can just hide underground or disguise myself as a farmer.

"Like you said, now we're in a war where millions of people have already been killed. If I stay here, it would be a life worse than death. But I promise I'll be back soon. Until then, just stay alive with the children. The People's Republic and our People's Army will never be defeated."

"I don't need your promise," said Mother. "If you can return that quickly, everything will be fine when you come home." But she must have had a premonition, because she trailed behind my father, who had picked up his rucksack and was already leaving the house. "Let's save our promises for later," she said. "How will I get through all this with the children . . . ?"

Father turned around. "Of course, I could be delayed," he said, "but what I said still holds. Whatever it takes, you and the kids just stay alive. No need to work hard and be frugal to get the kids an education. A bourgeois education will be useless, anyway, for a life in the People's Republic. Just stay alive—no more, no less."

By then the whole family, except for my baby brother— he was still nursing then, and asleep—was standing in the courtyard. Through the open gate, we could see a Soviet truck covered in a camouflage tarp and a few soldiers standing around, keeping guard. The back of the truck was already more than half full of people wearing clothes like my father's. My mother had wiped away her tears, but when she saw the others in the truck, she quietly followed behind Father with a look of resignation.

"Now, go inside," said Father. "Goodbye, kids. Listen to your mother." His voice was calm, like a man leaving for a trip to some not-too-distant place. He looked back at us before he climbed into the back of the truck, helped up by a young soldier.

Mother said nothing. Maybe she couldn't speak because she was overcome by emotion. My sister and I couldn't find a word to say during that sudden parting. We just kept clinging to Mother's dress, side by side.

Just before the truck pulled away, Father looked down at us for the last time and then furtively glanced up at the sky. I instinctively followed his gaze and looked up. It was an early autumn sky, clear and dazzling blue. Mother went back inside the courtyard after the truck had disappeared into the distance. She locked the front gate and crouched down in the courtyard sobbing, all the tears she had been holding back finally pouring forth. . . .

The next day, my brother arrived earlier than I expected. We hadn't set a specific time, but I assumed he would come around ten at the earliest, so I'd gotten up at eight and taken my time getting ready. By nine I had just washed my face and was about to go down to the restaurant when there was a knock at the door. It was Mr. Kim, and standing behind him, my brother.

I had worried endlessly about that first moment of our meeting. I had never seen him before in my life, and now he was nearly forty years old—and no doubt filled with the natural enmity that exists between half-brothers. I had no idea what to say to him, or even if I could address him informally.

But the moment I saw him, as he hesitantly entered the room following Mr. Kim, I realized that all my worries had been pointless. His face was very familiar, reminiscent of my father's—whose face had faded from memory, leaving only a shape and complexion I recalled with the help of a few old photos—and he also looked like my younger brother, who was still nursing when Father left, who grew up without him and died tragically before the age of forty. My half-brother's proportions were like those of my eldest son, who was in the army and whose slightly curved spine and long torso were unique to our family. The only odd thing about my half-brother was his suit, which looked like South Korean high fashion from the seventies.

He walked in with a hard expression, but looked shocked when he saw me. From the way his features softened afterward, I was certain he was having the same reaction I was. He didn't know what to do or what to say to me.

"Since he's your older brother, more than ten years your senior, you should greet him with a formal bow," said Mr. Kim. His instruction was a great help, and even made my first words to my brother easier. I replied to his formal bow with a half bow of my own, and since Mr. Kim had made it clear that I was older, I could address my younger brother informally.

"I've heard it already," I said, "but how do you write your name?" What I meant was what Chinese characters did he use. When I had first heard my brother's name from Mr. Kim, I thought my father had followed family tradition in selecting the Chinese characters for a son's name, but then I wondered if my father would have followed this naming convention for his second family, since it would have been a relic of feudal times. I had resolved to ask my brother when we met—but it hadn't been my intention for these to be the first words I spoke to him. I think he thought I was simply asking his name.

"It's Hyeok. I am called Yi Hyeok."

"I was asking you the Chinese characters, not your name," I said. "And you shouldn't use your surname when giving your name to your older brother . . . Hyeok—that's the character for 'red,' isn't it? Written with the 'fire' radical and two *jeoks*?"

"That's right."

"And do your brothers and sisters also have single character names?"

"No. My older sister and the youngest have two-character
names."

"Then they must have a *hui* or a *seop*."

"That's right. My sister is Munhui and my younger brother
is Museop."

At that point something like dread surged through my
heart. My father had been a loyal communist. He could aban-
don his young wife and three children in a burning city during wartime, yet he could not give up the old clan tradition
in naming his children!

"Do people still use traditional naming conventions in
North Korea?"

My brother simply stared at me, probably dumbfounded at
why I was so interested in names. I repeated my question,
confused by his silence, and stood there staring at him when
Mr. Kim suddenly realized the source of our mutual incom-
prehension and stepped in.

"You know—shared Chinese characters for the names of
family members. They used to use it in the old days in the
North, but I don't think it's used much these days."

"Oh," said my brother, finally understanding. "Nobody
does that anymore. We didn't use shared characters, either."

I suppressed the emotion building up in my chest, and
explained our family's naming practices at length. "The
naming tradition doesn't just use shared Chinese characters. It usually incorporates the five elements as generational
markers. It's different for each clan, but for us the order of
elements for the generations is earth, metal, water, wood, and

fire. We use *gyu* for earth, *hyeon* for metal, *ho* for water, *byeong* for wood, and *seop* or *hui* for fire. But it's possible not to use the characters and still mark the elements in each generation. For instance, the character for our generation is either *seop* or *hui*, but if you have a single character name, you can use one that includes the fire radical, *hwa*, in it or indicate it by using four dots under the character. So, you and all your siblings have names that follow the tradition exactly. I'm guessing, but if Father named your kids, their names probably have the Chinese character *gyu* or have the earth radical, *to*, in them."

When I noticed the puzzled expression on Mr. Kim's face, I quickly changed the subject. "Oh, I should have asked this first. How did Father pass away?"

"He had colon cancer. He died at the People's Hospital in Gimchaek." My brother's eyes became suddenly red and glistened as he said this. My own eyes stung for the first time since hearing news of my Father's death.

"Colon cancer," I said. "Did he go peacefully?"

"We have a relative at the hospital—Uncle Gyeongho, who came up from the South together with Father during the war. He took good care of Father. He was in a coma for a couple of days, so he didn't suffer that much."

My brother sounded like he was about to sob, but though my eyes stung and my vision was blurred, I wasn't feeling feel genuine sorrow. I wondered how my brother could come to tears reminiscing about my father nearly a year after his death, and part of me felt alienated for not being able to do the same although I was also his son. I was sufficiently detached to be preoccupied by something that had little to do with

Father's death. Uncle Gyeongho had graduated from a vocational high school during the Japanese occupation and worked at a bank before defecting to the North—so how had he become a doctor?

"That's good," I said. "What was the exact date he died? As the eldest son, I need to know so I can perform the rituals for the anniversary rite."

"He means your father's memorial ceremony," said Mr. Kim, like a dutiful interpreter.

Only then did my brother grasp my meaning. "It's August 21st and March 18th."

For a moment I wondered how there could be two dates, but then I understood. Father's birthday was March 18th. It seemed they held memorial services on the deceased's birthday in the North. There was a similar confusion for a while when we talked about the formalities of the memorial rites. My brother didn't know about the ancestral shrine, the ancestral tablet, and the mourning period. It seemed that the rituals in the North were more like Christian ceremonies and not like the traditional Confucian ceremonies we had in the South.

"Since you don't have an ancestral shrine for the tablet, I suppose I can attend to Father's spirit," I said. "I should be able to observe the anniversaries and the first and fifteenth-day services each month."

For the first time, I felt a strong antagonism emanating from my brother. His eyes flashed with indignation. "Then, do you mean you're taking the memorial services away from us?" The anger in his voice was unmistakable.

"No, I'm not taking away the memorial services. It's just that yours are like commemorations—like a birthday. All I'm saying is that we will hold a traditional Confucian service separately. Our family doesn't take these things lightly. Our clan is well respected in the Yeongnam area, and I'm descended from twelve generations of first sons. If we were a minor clan, I could easily have been the leader of the head family. How could I not observe Father's memorial while I'm offering services to eleven ancestors before him? Even if I wanted to leave him out, the clan wouldn't stand for it."

I went on to talk about our ancestors, the one who had the title of Minister bestowed on him posthumously, the one who was Magistrate of Andong, the one who served as Prefect of Uiryeong. Then I looked over at Mr. Kim. He had been doing a good job as interpreter until now, but this time he found it difficult. He struggled to explain to my brother that *yangban* families considered memorials very important and that the rituals have to be performed properly by the firstborn. But there was still a strong glint of resentment in my brother's eyes. I was confused by his hostility but also curious.

"I heard that you don't believe in things like ghosts or spirits," I said.

"Do you?" asked my brother. "From what I've heard, brother, you people in the South have practically turned into Yankees and don't believe in all that stuff."

He had just called me "brother" for the first time, but I wasn't moved because I was in too much of a hurry to defuse his resistance—more powerful than I had expected—in any way I could.

"It depends on the individual," I said. "But I believe in those things. Not out of superstition, but scientifically. I don't know if it's the right terminology, but you must know about the conservation of mass, momentum, and energy. I think the spirit is consciousness embodied in the mind while the body is alive, and the mind's activity is expressed as motion and energy. So if the matter that constitutes our bodies changes form but doesn't disappear after death, then why would consciousness disappear? There's the issue of whether you would retain your memories and identity, but I don't think it matters either way. If the spirit is connected to the mind before death, as many religions believe, then what gods would care about us more than the spirits of our ancestors would? Even if the mind disintegrates and is reassembled, like the body after death, what's the harm in paying respect to the spirits of the ancestors who brought our bodies into being? I believe the principles of feng shui—the resonance of life force in a landscape—can also apply to the spirits of our ancestors. So I perform the ceremonies not just as remembrances but as religious rituals."

I had no idea how absurd I must have sounded as I went on and on, summarizing my views on ancestral rites. My brother's expression softened a bit—perhaps he understood some of what I said—but it was hardly a sign of agreement.

I felt defensive. "What are you so upset about?" I asked bluntly. "You seem to have a problem with my wanting to perform the rites for Father."

My brother was equally blunt. "You appear out of nowhere, and it seems to me that you're strutting around like you're the only real son."

It was the inevitable hostility of a half-brother over the issue of legitimacy—something I felt myself after meeting him. But his frankness was somewhat of a consolation, and I wasn't as injured by it as I could have been. Instead, I was able to regard him calmly—the rules of kinship gave me the advantage, since I was the first son of my father's first wife. I could let my younger brother be the touchier one.

My sense of calm allowed me to change the subject and display benevolence as I promised to include all their names and dates of birth in our clan's genealogical record—not only those of my half-siblings but of their mother as well. My brother wasn't familiar with this practice, but he was tolerant. Only a hint of annoyance remained as he humored me by writing down the names and birth dates in my pocket notebook.

This time it was my turn to be upset as I silently read what he was writing. *Kang Myeongsun, of the Jinju clan, born June 2nd, 1930. Munhui, female, born August 17th, 1955* . . . I couldn't help but imagine the nature of my father's second marriage and his relationship with his second wife.

If the first child, Munhui, was born in 1955, Father's second marriage must have happened around 1954. My brother's mother, Kang Myeongsun, was only twenty-four at the time, which meant she was probably a virgin and not likely to be a widow or a divorcee. My father, who defected to the North in his prime at thirty-six, didn't marry again for almost four years, waiting until he was nearly forty. At least he had observed the minimum courtesy toward the wife he had left behind in the South. In those days, prostitution was strictly forbidden in the North, and even dating was not freely permitted, so if this was her first marriage, there would have been nothing against Kang Myeongsun making a proper wife, even if she came from the lower classes and had a poor education. In any case, she had been with my father for nearly forty years by the time he died—three times longer than my father had been with my mother in the South.

Who would accuse my father of unfaithfulness or immorality for his fruitful remarriage under those circumstances? Who could insult such a second wife and her three children by calling them a lowly concubine and her brood of bastards? Perhaps the thirteen-year marriage in the South was just a painful, fading memory for my father, and to his new family in the North my mother and her three children were merely a scar he bore, a wound that would not heal.

"Do you happen to have picture of your family?" I asked as my brother handed my notebook back. "I'm curious to see everybody—your siblings and your mother."

My brother hesitated, but then he produced his wallet and took a picture out of it. The six people in the family photo were smiling happily with a seaside beach in the background. My brother wasn't in the photo, probably because he was the one who had taken it. It looked like a happy time from Father's later years, and except for a girl in her mid-twenties—who reminded me of my older sister in Daegu when she was unmarried—the other children were all young.

I studied the photograph closely, and I felt something like envy as I suddenly remembered my mother—her hard life, doing needlework until she was past fifty, raising the three of us without a father, always exhausted from her responsibilities. Father, naturally, and the three children in the photo all looked familiar, but the face of his second wife was entirely alien to me—it was dark and ruddy, with a strong nose. She had a healthy physique, big-boned and sturdy. She looked entirely incompatible with my father, who had the elegant features of an intellectual.

It was that incompatibility that made me ask my next question. "Did you hear any stories about how your parents got married?"

My brother just looked at me for a moment. He answered without emotion, "I heard that when Father was teaching at Wonsan Agriculture College, Mother was one of his students. It was after she had come back from the South, where she was all the way down at the Nakdong River fighting as a woman warrior in the People's Army. They said they got married after they met again at the Yeoldu 3,000 Li Field in Mundeok."

"The Yeoldu 3,000 Li Field in Mundeok? Why did Father go there?"

"It was by the order of the Party. He ended up working on the irrigation project there in 1954. I was born in Mundeok."

"A college professor working at a construction site? He majored in agricultural economics, and they had him doing construction on an irrigation project? Did you ever hear why?"

Then I had a sudden realization. I had finally solved a puzzle that had always bothered me about the time after Father's defection to the North. Nineteen fifty-four was the year the Southern Labor Party faction was purged. My father had been a member of that party—he was probably implicated in something, removed from his professorship, and sent to work on the irrigation project site at Uiju. That would explain the contradictory reports I had heard from two relatives. One, who was sent south as a spy and arrested just after the cease-fire, had said my father was a professor at Wonsan Agriculture College. The other had defected in the sixties after being sent South and had been making the rounds as an anticommunist speaker. He had insisted that my father was an engineer at some place whose name I had never heard before. My brother did not seem to know any of this.

"Why? It was the Party's orders."

"In the letter I got in the mid-eighties, I heard he was at the Agricultural Science Institute. Was that true?"

"That's where he worked until he died."

"Then why did he live in Cheongjin?"

"We've been living in Cheongjin since I was in high school. We lived in Mundeok while Father was as an engineer at the Irrigation Project office. Then while he was re-educated at Songdo College of Politics and Economy, we lived in Pyongyang for about three years. We moved to Cheongjin after that."

If I had kept digging, I could have learned more about what my father had to endure after going north, but I changed the subject because I didn't want to agitate my brother without good reason. But I ended up tangling the thread of our conversation, which had been playing out quite smoothly.

"So, how are you all getting by?" I asked. I meant it simply as a friendly question, to show my concern for those who shared my blood, but for some reason this inquiry made my brother noticeably hostile. The look in his eyes suggested that he had been anticipating this turn all along.

"What do you mean?" he said. "Do you want me to tell you how we're starving and can't get enough corn gruel to eat?"

"Why would I want to do that? I'm just curious, since we're relatives who will be relying on each other when reunification comes. How are you all doing?"

"My older sister is married to a diplomat and she's living abroad. My younger sister married a leader of the Light Industry Committee last year. My younger brother is a teacher, and my youngest brother started at Pyongyang Foreign Language College this year. I belong to the organization branch of the Gimchaek Enterprise Consortium Party Committee. I don't know how you see it, but the five of us are doing quite well."

My brother's tone was somewhat sarcastic, so I replied with an irony of my own. "Like Father said in his letter, it sounds like your family got more from your country than you gave it. I'm glad. I know we shouldn't believe everything we hear, but I heard that life is hard in the North, so I was concerned."

My brother gave me another jab. "We heard you were having a lot of hardships in the South, so when the National Security Bureau first brought news about you, we were honestly surprised. At one time Father said the family in the South was probably all massacred. . . . I wonder why the lackeys of the Yankee imperialists were so generous to you. . . ."

It sounded to me like his real question was how I myself had come to be one of those imperialist lackeys. To be honest, I had never, until that moment, felt the need to defend the system of government I live under, but once I heard my brother's question, I felt suddenly compelled to champion that system, as if I were a representative at a South-North summit.

"What Father said was true. Actually, our whole family *was* almost massacred, and we did suffer a lot. We often went hungry and we were discriminated against countless times as we grew up. I still have the bad habit of overeating because of the years we starved. I thought I should eat a lot whenever there was food, since we never knew when we'd be able to eat again. And we were always under close surveillance. When I was in college a detective would check up on me once a month, so I had a hard time getting work even as a private tutor. Who wanted a tutor with an anticommunist detective tailing him? We had to endure that sort of hounding for twenty more years, even after I was a full-time lecturer at my university. It finally ended in 1982, by special order of the military regime. The oppression of those who were guilty by association seemed to stop then."

I hadn't intended it when I began my story, but once I started telling it, something suddenly welled up in my heart, and it was hard for me to go on. The wounds I bore from the first half of my life because of the legal tradition of guilt by association came back to me all at once, stirring up all the anger and sorrow from those days, things that had settled into the depths of my consciousness during the long time I had repressed them. These weren't emotions I wanted to harbor for very long—so I collected myself and tried to be faithful to my initial intention of making contact with my brother.

"In fact, my life isn't all that great now. My home is a 1,300-square-foot apartment that's barely larger than a chicken coop, and my car—I was only able to move up to a Korean midsize when I became a full-time professor. This ten-day trip with all the extra expenses is costing me almost half a month's pay.

"The rich people live in palatial mansions and drive around in big foreign luxury cars. Some of those bastards go all the way to Hawaii or Australia just to play golf, but I had to bide my time cautiously, keeping a low profile and enduring humiliation just to live the way I do now.

"I could never join any of those typical demonstrations when I was a university student, and in the eighties, when every two-bit intellectual was shouting 'Nationalism! and Progress!' I wore my label of conservative reactionary like a badge of honor."

My honesty, as I told my story, came mostly from bitterness. It was as if I were saying, "We are poor because our housekeeper is poor, our gardener is poor, and our chauffeur is poor. . . ." There was an ironic double edge to it—I could have been implicitly bragging about my wealth. This was a petty reaction on my part to my brother's obviously embellished description of their lives. But as I summarized the tragedy and humiliation we endured after Father's departure, I surprised myself, and by the time I was through, my voice was trembling, and instead of injuring my brother as I had wanted, my bitterness wound up evoking his sympathy.

"So you did suffer. When I was young I would see Father crying by himself once in a while, and now I know why."

I was surprised by his response, and a bit self-conscious, but since I had begun, I kept pushing forward.

"I had some money to spare recently, so I bought some land in our hometown, but it doesn't compare to the vast tracts of land our family used to own when they cultivated rice. I got a quarter of an acre to build a villa out in the country, but it would be more accurate to call it a cottage."

My brother replied with his own indignation. "I'd heard that corporate toadies own thousands of acres of land and scenic places are all packed with their country villas where they carry on with their young whores." He still didn't get it—and I had no choice but to throw up my hands. My approach had obviously been too sophisticated for someone so naïve.

Mr. Kim must have sensed that something was amiss, because he stepped in at that point to rescue me. "From what Professor Ryu said, I understand that you're quite rich by our standards," he said. "He told me that you were worth more than one million U.S. dollars and that professors in the South enjoy more respect and much higher salaries than they do up here."

The mention of "one million U.S. dollars" seemed to stun my brother. His expression of sympathy disappeared, and for a moment he couldn't hide the confusion on his face. Then he turned red with indignation, and sensing that he had been insulted, he breathed heavily. "Then you mean to tell me you've just been bragging about your money all this time?"

"Not at all," I said. But for some reason, my face grew hot as if I'd just been caught in an underhanded trick. "Those things just came up as I was talking about my life. What Mr. Kim here says is true, but in the South what I have is nothing worth bragging about."

To hide my embarrassment, I quickly produced the liquor and food I had brought. Before leaving Seoul, I had stopped in my hometown to pick up a bottle of Andong *soju*, chestnuts, and dried dates and persimmons. I had planned to ask my brother to make an offering of them to Father's spirit, but I also expected the ritual to help bring us closer, and if there was an uncomfortable pause in our conversation or if something wasn't going well, I could use the gifts like a good luck charm.

I tried hard to act naturally as I opened my suitcase and produced the large ceramic jug of *soju*.

"This is Andong *soju*," I said. "Please offer it to Father in my place." I stressed the word *Andong* as I presented it to my brother.

But my brother, still annoyed, didn't respond as I expected. "We have plenty of good liquor in North Korea, too," he said brusquely as he took it, unable to decline. "Why bother bringing it from so far . . . ?"

When he saw the dried fruit and nuts I had brought, he really became indignant. "How expensive are chestnuts and dates that you brought all this with you? Did you hear we don't even have chestnuts or dates for a memorial table up here?"

My brother's vehement reaction offered me a chance to console him without feeling superior. "This *soju* was made with water from where Father was born and raised," I said. "I wanted to bring local rice wine originally, but I thought it might turn, so I chose the *soju* instead. No matter how good the liquor is here in the North is, could there be any sweeter liquor than this for Father? These chestnuts and dates, too. The chestnuts were picked in the back hills, and the dates were picked from the hill with the ancestral graves. The persimmons were peeled and dried in Solshil, just over the pass.

"They're all things that grew out of the land Father played on when he was young, the land he returned to once in a while in his youth, but could never see again once he went north. He longed for that place for over forty years but closed his eyes without being able to walk there again." At this point I choked up in spite of myself and had to stop, but by then my brother had become solemn and was listening in silence.

"Since you don't have an ancestral shrine, please offer it at his grave," I said. "It's not exactly in keeping with the rules of filial piety, but . . ."

"I understand, brother." His voice bore not even a shadow of animosity—we were undeniably brothers again.

After that, my brother said he had other business to tend to that day and made ready to leave. Though he knew I was planning to leave Yanji the next day on an eleven o'clock flight, he didn't even mention whether he would come and see me once more.

If that was the case—goodbye without knowing if we would ever see each other again—I was not about to let him go. And though he had been in a rush to leave at first, he must have sensed my feelings, because now he also seemed reluctant. I suggested we say goodbye after having lunch together, and that was agreeable to him. I didn't want to offend him again. I left the choice of restaurant to Mr. Kim, and he picked a modest Korean place nearby.

While we hadn't exactly been connecting as brothers—perhaps because it was the first time we had met—the drinks we had at lunch had a surprising effect, renewing the bond between us. It was only beer, but my brother gulped down glass after glass as I poured for him, and I couldn't help thinking how blood was thicker than water, how a blood relation could not be denied. I watched as his face reddened slightly from the alcohol.

"Brother, you drink just like Father," he said. "Calmly, without making a face, like you're drinking water. You even laugh louder when you drink, just like he did. He left when you were little, you couldn't possibly have seen him drink. . . ."

"I think I remember hearing him laugh in the men's study. . . . Are we that much alike?"

Father had left when I was nine, but I had probably heard the sound of his laughter at least a couple of years earlier. The year before the war, he was hiding underground, so he wouldn't have had occasion to laugh like that, and after the war began, there would have been no chance to sit around drinking and laughing because he was always busy as far as I knew. I didn't remember any laughter in the house the year before the war or during it—all I had was the memory of a thought or a feeling: *Father must be drinking with his friends in the study.* And yet this shared memory brought me closer to my brother and lowered my guard. I felt that I couldn't let him go without apologizing for the animosity I had shown toward him in the hotel. I had to explain myself.

"What I said earlier—please forgive me if it upset you. I wanted to tell you that I live comfortably, not brag about my wealth. Just take it to mean that things were hard in the past but they're all right now and you don't need to worry. Not everyone in South Korea is money crazy."

What I told him wasn't exactly a lie. I had worried about their lives from time to time before meeting my brother, so it wasn't unreasonable to assume that the other family might have been concerned about my family as well.

But what I said at the end caused a new shame to well up in my heart. Though I pretended I was a reluctant participant— led on by my wife with my hands tied—there were few acts I was innocent of among the large-scale corruptions the media had criticized so vociferously when the Kim Young-sam government began its reforms. When it came to the real estate market, I had benefited from many forms of corruption, only on a lesser scale.

The apartment we were living in—I had gotten it cheaply because my wife had bought it under the name of her older sister, who was still living alone. My country house on the east coast was now quite an expensive estate, but my wife had bought it dirt cheap ten years earlier when it was a farmhouse at the mouth of the harbor—we acquired it by falsely claiming it would remain a farm. I bought the 3,000 *pyeong* paddy field in my hometown not just under someone else's name but by getting a dubious loan. I had gotten countless bank loans for which I did not qualify, loans that were practically fraudulent, because I had a personal friend behind the desk. This was the real truth behind my "one million dollars," which would have been impossible to amass on my professor's salary. And yet my brother accepted my explanations as the truth.

"Don't worry about it," he said. "It was small-minded of me. Let's let it go." Then, after a moment's hesitation, he produced a small silk pouch from the shoulder bag he had been carrying. He wore a solemn expression now, as if announcing that it was his turn to reveal something honestly.

Mr. Kim became nervous, sensing what might be in the pouch. "Why did you bring that?" he asked.

"Before he passed away, Father told me to give it to him."

My brother opened the pouch and produced a well-polished medal. It must have been very precious from the way he handled it, but it didn't look all that important, though it was obviously well cared for. I had visited Berlin in 1989, when the Wall came down, and bought an East German medal for twenty marks. What my brother presented to me looked similar.

"This is the National First Class Flag medal," he said. "Among all the medals Father earned for his lifelong tireless work for the Republic, this is the highest honor. At the peak of the struggle for agricultural development in the sixties, the Great Leader himself acknowledged Father's ten years of public service in leading the irrigation project at Yeoldu 3,000 Li Field. The Great Leader pinned this medal on Father in person."

My brother said this looking straight at me. Had it been earlier in our meeting, I would probably have compared the status of a college professor with that of an irrigation engineer, then pondered Father's hard life and the problem of changing one's career after the age of forty. But it was different now. I think I understood his intention.

The moment I heard my brother's words I was moved more than he could have imagined. Father had instructed him to deliver the most precious thing he had earned in his life to me, to his family in the South. He was sending us his most precious possession with the hope that it would be a small consolation for all that we had suffered because of him. But what moved me just as much was what my brother said next.

"My family gave me a lot of grief when I decided to bring this to you. They wanted to know why I was giving such a valuable thing to a South Korean puppet of the American imperialists. But I won in the end. First of all, it was Father's wish. When I said that we couldn't know what sort of person you were until I met you, they all backed off."

"So, now that you've met me, what do you think?" I asked. There was an involuntary quaver in my voice.

"You are my older brother," he said. "No—you are Father's firstborn son. I don't know if you're a puppet of the American imperialists, but you don't look like a man who would disgrace this medal. . . ." He presented the silk pouch to me with both hands, as if he were performing a solemn ritual.

Suddenly I thought of the gloomy landscape across the Tumen River. We had finished our lunch, but I didn't know if my brother had planned all along to end our meeting with the ceremony of delivering the medal.

Without checking first with my brother, I asked Mr. Kim, "Where was that place by the Tumen River—where we went with Professor Ryu last year?"

"You mean Haishan? Across from our Changbaek Hyeon?"

"Yes, that sounds right. How long would it take to get there?"

"Round-trip, that would be about an hour."

I looked at my brother. "You said you had some business this afternoon, right? Is it something you really have to do?"

"Huh?"

"We're brothers," I said earnestly. "If we part like this, we don't know when we might see each other again. Could you spare me just two more hours?"

My brother, finally understanding my meaning, glanced at the wall clock. His expression was ambivalent—I couldn't read it. His forehead creased in thought for a moment, and then he asked me, calmly, "How do you plan to use those two hours?"

"Could you come to Haishan with me? Just a few moments, by the Tumen River . . ."

"What do you plan to do there?"

"There's a traditional ceremony called *mangje*, 'Mourning from Afar.' When an ancestor's burial site can't be found because of war or a natural disaster, we get as close as we can to the burial site and make offerings in that direction. I should visit Father's grave and offer my tears of mourning there, but your Republic is blocking the way. Since I can't go to his grave, what about the two of us going to the Tumen River and offering a *mangje*, side by side? I would like to pour a drink and bow in front of Father's spirit."

By the time I'd finished explaining, my brother face showed that he had made up his mind. "All right," he said. "I'll make the time."

So we ended up making an unplanned trip to the banks of the Tumen River. Mr. Kim had enough sense not to try and accompany us to the *mangje*. He helped us buy the items we would need at a nearby market—fish and fruit for a simple offering—then put us in a cab driven by a Korean Chinese driver and went on his way. I figured he planned to settle his fee with me that night at the hotel.

Unlike the streets of Yanji, the banks of the Tumen showed almost no signs of change. The gloomy North Korean mountains across the river stretched out under a sky filled with a strange yellowish haze, and mid-slope, the giant billboards

I had seen two years earlier still read "Chollima Movement" and "Rapid Deployment." The Tumen River was also the same, disappointingly shallow and tainted by the pollution coming from upstream.

We didn't have a proper straw mat, so we found a spot along the river where the grass was thick and set out the memorial table on sheets of newspaper. Though I knew it would be of little use to my brother, I explained to him the basics for setting out the offerings: *Red East White West*—the rule for placing red fruit to the east and white fruit to the west; *East Head West Tail*—the rule for aligning the fish offering; and finally, *Dates Chestnuts Persimmons Pears*—our clan's unique sequence for fruits and nuts.

"I will have to make the offering. If I had my way, I'd offer ceremonial rice and three rounds of drinks, but since we're making do under these conditions it'll be enough to offer fish, fruit and a single cup. You pour the *soju*."

Though it was mourning from afar in a foreign land, we did it as solemnly as if we were at Father's ancestral grave. The taxi driver watched us with amusement from the riverbank and the occasional passerby glanced at us curiously, but I didn't feel at all self-conscious. I must have been moved by a religious fervor beyond the demands of tradition. My brother, also affected by my fervor, performed the role of assistant well—not once did I need to remind him about the ceremonial details.

The real sorrow of mourning finally came as I emptied the glass and made the last bow toward North Korea. I began to weep, my tears flowing uncontrollably, as I lowered my head for the final half-bow and glimpsed the landscape of my Father's Republic—bleak and gloomy under the pall of yellow dust—a summary of my Father's life. It pierced my heart.

My father was born the only son of an ambitious mother who was widowed early. His youth was legendary, full of stories that were probably part fiction: an ambitious adolescence, the brilliant accomplishment of studying in Tokyo during the Japanese occupation, the young ideologue. Though he endured occasional hardships, during his thirty-six years in the South there were no foreshadowings of failure.

But his forty years in the North—how must he have looked back on them during the final moments of his life? Of course, Father was guided by the dazzling light of his ideology. He once said to Mother that he would be happy to be a janitor at an elementary school, or a nameless factory worker, if only the Republic in his heart could become a reality. But would such a thing ever come to pass? The wife and three young children he left behind in the conflagration of the South must have torn at his heart like a wound that would never heal. He had to survive by changing careers at the age of forty and then enduring ten years of bone-breaking labor. An economics professor demoted to site engineer—no different from a laborer—he became chief engineer and then an irrigation expert, something entirely unrelated to his field. *Even if, in the end, he closed his eyes with satisfaction, I have the right to declare his life a failure and cry for him.* . . . I said this to myself as I fumbled around, unable to control my sudden tears.

When I was young, whenever there was some alarm caused by tensions along the DMZ, I imagined Father as a general, sitting high on a white horse, leading the People's soldiers south. When news about North Korea became generally available and the names of the top one hundred in the power elite were mentioned, I could not find Father's name among them. I immediately concluded this was because the source of information was unreliable. During my days as a teaching assistant, I got my hands on a document about the history of the communist revolution in South Korea, and when I couldn't find my father's name on the list of Southern Labor Party members—or even on the list of fringe organizations that were so common—I had no doubt that it was because he used a pseudonym, a common practice among the major figures in those days. There was only one basis for my beliefs: if Father was not among the greats in the North, I could not rationalize the pain and suffering that Mother and I and my three siblings had to endure. And now this same logic became the basis for my right to mourn Father's failure. . . .

That's what I thought, anyway—that I was mourning my father's failures—but I gradually realized I was crying for myself, for my past pain and suffering, now beyond the chance of redemption, and for my twisted psyche, which I had neglected, vowing to survive until the arrival of that "someday." As I became more emotional, I recalled the vehement criticisms I had endured from the People's and Nationalist historians in the eighties, and though I had handled them confidently at the time, they now cut me to the quick. I was a reactionary historian—I had mistaken the neo-imperialist army for liberators and neocolonialism for a close alliance, all the while gorging on the sweet fruits of an economic prosperity created by military dictators who were merely pawns of the developed nations.

I cried for an absurdly long time, but my brother stood by me without a sound, until, by and by, I collected myself and gave a polite cough to signal the end of our mourning. When I wiped away my tears as we cleared the offerings, I saw tears glistening on my brother's cheeks. This time he must have been overcome by my inexplicable sadness. I felt an even stronger blood kinship with him at that moment, and I sat down on the newspapers we had spread.

"Did you know that by drinking the liquor offered to our ancestors you receive their blessing?" I asked him, raising the glass that still held some *soju*. "It's called *eumbok*. Come, brother, let's each have a glass of *eumbok*."

As he took the glass, my brother said something unexpected. "Wasn't this called 'Jebiwon Soju' in the old days?"

"How do you know that?"

"I think I heard it Father say it when he was alive." Then he picked up a chestnut to eat and asked, with a thin smile, "Are there still lots of chestnut trees up in the back hills?"

"Nearly half of them were replaced with improved breeds in the sixties, but the hills are still full of them. Now how do you know about that?"

"I know about Pine Valley, too. And Stone Creek, and Red Screen Mountain, and the place for watching fish . . ." He went on, as if he'd been all over my hometown. My heart was stung again as I saw, in my brother, Father's forty years of intense homesickness. Even then, I was still keeping score, not to be outdone in this exchange of sentimentality, and I replied a little too quickly:

"Is Cheongjin still that cold and windy? They called it 'sand winds,' I think, the cold wind that makes your bone marrow ache. And is there still a field of gravel that stretches for ten *li*? And the smoke and dust spewing from the Gimchaek iron foundry?"

"How you know about those places?"

"It's the place where Father and you all live. How could I not be interested? I know about Two Swallows Mountain, Camel Mountain, and Moving Castle Creek, too."

My brother looked as if he were about take my hands and burst into tears. I had been calculating, not malicious, but seeing him respond so innocently made me feel guilty, and I became careful about what I said.

The fact that we shed tears together, bowing side by side in front of Father's spirit (though from afar), greatly lessened my initial urgency. Until that moment I had been in a near manic rush to learn about my brother. It was the pressure of our first meeting that made me more calculating and talkative than usual. But now I felt content, and I let my brother carry the conversation. I didn't think he was much of a talker, but between all the alcohol and our brotherly intimacy, he was able to ask, one by one, questions he must have been suppressing all along.

"South Korea," he said. "What's it really like there?"

"There are lots of ugly things about it, but people still manage to live there."

"What's it like living down there? I'm confused. If you look at *The Truth About South Korea* material the Party hands out, it sounds miserable. But that doesn't seem to be the case if you look at the people who've been abroad—they act pompous and are always whispering to each other. And what I heard after I got here last night . . ."

"At the moment, I think the South looks more affluent and luxurious than the North—but there's no guarantee it will last. Some say it's like being a sharecropper. I mean, like the overseer who exists between a tenant farmer and the land-owner. Some even compare it to the life of a concubine, to be blunt. Live the high life before you fall out of favor—borrow money to eat well and spend while you can . . ."

When I answered him that way, without hiding what was in my heart, my brother responded by saying something I found unexpectedly candid.

"I think I heard something like that, too. But sometimes I think that if we eventually have to recognize private property and live in a market economy, wouldn't it be better to be the landowner and not the tenant farmer? And if it's the path to becoming the landowner you want, wouldn't the share-cropper be closer than the tenant farmer? It's hard being a concubine, but the way I see it, a sharecropper has succeeded to some degree in a capitalist world. He's gained an advanta-geous position in the scheme of international exploitation."

"It's a bit surprising to hear you say that. Are there a lot of people in the North who think that way?" I couldn't help asking, because the tone of his argument seemed strange.

My brother looked a bit flustered. "Actually, it's something I heard from a friend in the International Economics Bureau. He's served abroad a bit as a vice secretary in trade relations. When I first heard it from him, it sounded quite reaction-ary. It just came to mind as I was listening to you. I wasn't testing you or anything."

"I think he only looked at the good side of the South Korean economy. Actually, that's probably just what the South wants with slogans like 'joining the ranks of developed nations,' 'globalization,' or 'import technology.' What is that except a desperate attempt to become the exploiter and not the exploited in the scheme of international exploitation? But it's not as easy as that."

"Still, you've done well up to now, haven't you? Especially if you look just at the economy . . ."

"You could say we've been managing, but every day now the cracks are beginning to show. The developed nations are holding us back—it's no joke—and the increased dependence that comes with development is a problem, too."

"You mean on the U.S.? I've heard about it, but is it so hard living in servitude to the Americans?"

My instincts told me to be wary at that point, but I was already in no mood to be guarded with my brother. I just exaggerated a bit about the concerns I had from time to time, based on hearsay. "There's the problem of political autonomy, but the truly serious problem is economic dependency. These days the political sanctions aren't as scary to us as economic threats backed by the enormous American market."

"Can't you just cut yourselves off from the Yankees and be self-sufficient like us?"

"In other words, you're saying we should be satisfied living in a shack in the hills, farming a few plots of land and living on millet and barley? I guess it's different now, but isn't that how you did it in the North until just recently? Did you like living like that?"

"I don't see why not. If you cultivate the spirit of self-reliance and work hard . . ." The tone of his words wasn't as confident as what I'd heard on North Korean television.

"I don't know," I said. "Even the Japanese, whose are at least ten times as strong as us in every respect, didn't have that kind of power. Look at how they tried to stand up to the Americans and ended up begging for mercy when they got whipped."

Just then, the taxi driver, who was walking back and forth on the levee waiting for us to finish, coughed loudly to remind us. It was fortuitous because we had finished most of the liquor and the conversation was beginning to touch on sensitive and complicated issues. I got to my feet first.

"Are you all right with time?" I asked.

My brother glanced down at his watch and suddenly looked anxious. "I have to get going," he said. "I can't believe how quickly the time . . ."

My brother gathered up the remaining offerings. It was only a few fruits, trimmed top and bottom, a few handfuls of chestnuts and dates, and some dried fish. But when it was wrapped up, the bundle seemed larger than the one we had brought. My brother's left shoulder sagged under the weight, so I offered a hand.

"It looks heavy. Give it to me. I'll carry it."

"It's all right. I'll carry it, brother." He switched the bundle over to his right hand. Maybe it was the liquor—but for a moment I had the illusion that I was back home, coming down from the ancestral graves with members of my clan after a memorial ceremony.

"You're not supposed to take this home with you," I explained. "The things used for an offering, the *eumbok*, should be distributed to a neighboring clan or the keeper of the gravesite. Is there anyone you could give this *eumbok* to? If not, why don't you give it to the driver?"

We continued to talk in the car on the way back to Yanji. My brother was clearly drunk—it was obvious by the way he was walking—but he must have been conscious of the driver. Now that it was no longer just the two of us, he seemed more careful about what he said.

"Brother, why are you like that in the South? I mean, about the nuclear issue. If we develop nuclear weapons, where would they go in the end? Unification will happen, eventually, and then the South becomes a nuclear power for free. So why are they dancing for the Yankees like they're puppets? Do they really think we'd fire our missiles at the South?"

When I seemed to doubt his unwavering faith in the North Korean regime, he resorted to peculiar rhetoric. "Up here in the North, the people are one with the land. If you look around Cheongjin, the Suseong River levee and Camel Mountain bomb shelter were built with the sweat of my labor when I was mobilized in high school. And there isn't a spot in the Ranam fields where you won't find my footprints from when I helped with transplanting rice. I can honestly say there's no place in that city, port, or railroad that I haven't personally laid my hands on. It's the same everywhere else. The people have nurtured every blade of grass, every single tree in the homeland with their own two hands."

It was to his credit that he didn't irritate me by singing the praises of the "Great Leader" or the "Dear Leader." By that point I hadn't the slightest desire to agitate my brother by criticizing his faith in his system. Whether it was genuine or just a conditioned parroting of indoctrination, I was relieved to see that he believed in the system he had to live in. I responded sympathetically.

When we reached downtown Yanji, I lapsed back into my original sense of urgency. I recalled that this meeting might be our last as well as our first, and that left me feeling as if we were overlooking a necessary part of a ritual.

There was a momentary pause in our conversation as the taxi turned down a street and we could see the hotel in the distance. "I leave tomorrow morning," I said. "Could we meet again?"

My brother, intoxicated by his own words, looked at me as if I'd startled him awake. "I don't know . . ." he said. "But I'll try to make time and stop by. Tonight or early tomorrow morning."

"If it's not possible, then this is it. If we say goodbye now, I wonder if we'll ever meet again." Once I said that, I regretted all the time we had wasted on useless chatter.

My brother must have felt the same. "We'll see each other again soon, don't you think? It won't be long until the day of unification."

I got the sense that he didn't really believe his own words. Then the hesitation I had felt on and off in my heart since we had met—which had been suppressed for a while by the intensity of the ceremonial offering—reasserted itself.

I had left Seoul with a small sum in U.S. dollars to give my brother. I knew that North Korea was suffering hard times, but judging from my brother's circumstances, he did not appear to be in desperate need. The money was also because I didn't know what sort of consequences he might have to bear for coming to see me.

But now that I had met him, I could not decide whether or not to offer him the money. I had put off this decision, then forgotten about it because of my brother's exceptional sensitivity to issues like the standard of living and material comforts. Now it had come up again.

While I was still vacillating, the taxi pulled up at the hotel. I quietly glanced at my brother's face, hoping to find some clue in his expression. He didn't notice. He looked at his watch and hurriedly got out of the car. Nowhere on his face was there an indication that he was expecting financial help from me. I considered asking him casually if he would accept a gift of money, but now there was no time left for that.

I got out of the taxi after him, having given up the idea of thrusting the envelope full of dollars into his hand. I gently grasped his hand instead. My brother was about to tell me something, but he winced and closed his mouth.

"If you can't come back, I guess this is goodbye," I said.

"I'll try my best to come again . . . if it's possible."

"No need to try too hard. Like you said, unification will come soon. Then we'll be able to see each other whenever we want."

I didn't know what he did as part of the Enterprise Consortium Party Committee, but my brother's hand was rougher than I expected. I took his other hand in mine and said goodbye. "Be well until we meet again. If there is such a thing as a spirit, Father's will be watching over all of you. Be careful about everything, and look after yourself."

It felt as if I had spent a long time with my brother, and now I was sending him off without any assurance that I would ever see him again.

His eyes glistened as if they were welling up with tears. "You be well, too, brother."

"Give my regards to our brothers and sisters," I said. Then, as if I'd made a grave decision, I added, "To Mother, too."

In the scenario I had choreographed so carefully and for so long after deciding to meet my brother, I had struggled with how I would refer to his mother. "Northern Mother," "New Mother," "Stepmother" . . . Finally, after meeting him, I was able to get by with an added modifier, "your mother," but now all the modifiers had flown away.

In ancient Confucian law there were exceptional cases when the taking of a second wife was permissible if certain criteria were met. To my modern rational thinking, it wasn't a problem to consider my brother's mother my mother, too. But I startled myself with how naturally the word "Mother" rolled off my tongue.

My brother immediately sensed this, too. He regarded me for a moment, his face now unclouded by drunkenness, and then he bowed his head in acceptance.

"Give our regards to our sister and nephews, too. And to Mother." He did not use a modifier either.

When I stepped into the hotel lobby, it was quite busy. A large tour group had just arrived. More than twenty men and women were sorting through the luggage to find their bags. From the amount of dialect I heard in their loud voices, it seemed that a group from the provinces had come for a tour of Mt. Baekdu.

There was a time when I was happy to see Korean tour groups while I was traveling abroad. In those days I would approach complete strangers and ask where they were from, and if I knew the sights of a particular city, I would even offer bits of friendly advice. But at some point I began to feel embarrassed by Korean tourists, meeting them became tiresome, and eventually I began to avoid them altogether.

That's how I felt that day. I didn't know who they were, but I disliked them just for the way they were dressed in gaudy colors and Western designer fashions—blue jeans, shorts, sneakers with famous brand names stitched on their tongues. The men all wore safari jackets, as if they were off to hunt tigers on Mt. Baekdu, and they all had cameras dangling under their chins—mostly Japanese camcorders. It looked like a group of married couples, and the women were probably housewives. They were showing off in their vulgar Western *skorts*—so short they might as well have been wearing hot pants.

And they were oblivious of others. The men stood around in clusters of three and four, talking loudly, not caring if they were in the way or making a nuisance of themselves, and the women sat on lobby sofas with their legs apart, exposing their pasty thighs as if they were masseuses in some Western film— or they lay with both legs outstretched on their bags, as if they were in their bedrooms at home. It was all too excessive, too arrogant, and it disgusted me.

I had no reason to reveal my inner feelings, so trying hard to maintain a blank expression, I was crossing the lobby to get to the elevator when someone followed me and asked, "How are you?" It sounded like the North Korean dialect common in Yanji.

When I turned to look, it was Mr. Reunification. I hadn't seen him for the past few days, though he was staying at the same hotel. His face was flushed. He must have sounded North Korean to me because he had spoken so politely, but he was dressed so formally that it was hard to believe he was a tourist like the others: gray suit, brown tie, and black leather shoes—the colors were all dignified.

"Oh, I'm fine," I said. "I heard you'd stayed behind. How is your work going?"

Something was off. The front of his suit and shirt was mottled with dried stains as if he had spilled something on himself and hastily wiped it off. When he came and stood next to me, I thought I smelled food.

He must have sensed what I was thinking. "Oh, you mean this?" he said. "The waiter spilled a plate when I was eating lunch . . ."

He wasn't very convincing. I wondered how the waiter had managed to have an accident over his head, of all places—there were also stains on his shoulders and shirt collar.

I didn't let on. "If you don't have another suit, leave it with the hotel right now," I said. "They can clean it for you by the time we leave. We're going to stay in Beijing another night, and you might want to go somewhere where you have to dress formally."

"I'll be fine. I'm going with everyone else to see the Imperial Garden and the Thirteen Ming Tombs so I'll just dress casually."

While he was trying hard to answer nonchalantly, the elevator door opened. We stepped inside and I casually pressed the button for 8, my floor. Mr. Reunification was about to press the button for his floor when he paused and suddenly looked at me.

"Is someone coming to see you?" he asked.

"Not at the moment." I thought of my appointment with Mr. Kim, but that wasn't until after dinner.

"What will you do in an empty room all by yourself?" Mr. Reunification said, lowering his voice. "The gang that went to Mt. Baekdu won't be back till after dark, so why don't we go up to the lounge and chat? You look like you've have had a bit to drink already, so . . . I'll buy you a beer, Professor Yi."

When he saw my surprise at his use of my title, he smiled and said, "I recognized you from the start. I'm a nobody myself, but I've been interested in history for a while. . . . You're Professor Yi of Hanil University, am I right?"

I still hadn't recovered my composure when the elevator stopped at the eighth floor. Mr. Reunification pushed the close button without even asking, then pressed the button for the lounge.

Unlike the downstairs coffee shop, the lounge was nearly deserted. I felt like Mr. Reunification's helpless prisoner as I took a seat with him by a window with a view. Actually, I doubt I could have stayed in my room by myself after saying goodbye to my brother—I probably would have gone up to the lounge anyway to drown my sorrows.

Mr. Reunification ordered three bottles of beer and some dry snacks without consulting me. Suddenly, he began muttering to himself with a bitter smile. "That grave robber must be in the middle of something about now. I should have gone back to the room and foiled him."

"What?"

"I'm talking about the businessman who stayed back here in Yanji with us. I heard you met him in the coffee shop, yesterday."

"Oh, the businessman. Yes, I did speak to him briefly, yesterday, but . . ."

"Businessman? What kind of rotten businessman? If that's business, then thieving and whoring must be business, too, Professor. Do you know why he came here? To smuggle out cultural treasures. The store he brags about in Insadong is just a front. He's a thief who made it big by looting tombs."

I finally recovered from the shock of realizing that Mr. Reunification had been playing dumb all this time when he had known all along who I was.

"Is that so?" I said. "But it can't be easy sneaking cultural treasures out of here. Smuggling's been a problem in China for so long, I'm sure customs is very strict about things like antiques." In my nervousness, I wanted to lapse back into my habit of dwelling on details.

"It's not their cultural treasures—those would be easily recognized. The things he's smuggling out aren't Chinese cultural treasures."

"Don't they classify Goguryeo and Balhae artifacts as Chinese cultural treasures?" I was thinking that the businessman must have been eyeing relics from the ancient Korean kingdoms that were now Chinese territory, but I was entirely wrong.

"That's not what I meant. I meant Yi Dynasty white ceramics and ancient classical paintings."

"Can there be enough of those things to make it worthwhile to come all the way from Korea? You know, the people who settled here mostly trickled in because they had nowhere else to live during the Japanese occupation. They were destitute. They traveled thousands of *li*, practically begging all the way, and I don't think that they would have carried valuable ceramics or scroll paintings."

"I think he's smuggling things out of North Korea, not here in Yanji. Honestly, I was shocked. He's done it many times."

I thought I understood. If they could smuggle people like Mr. Kim Hanjo out, why couldn't they smuggle out some antiques?

"How?" I asked.

"From what I gathered, sharing a room for the past two days, I think it's like this. First, he picks people with family in North Korea or who travel in and out on business. He pays them a lot up front and sends them in. They buy up anything that looks old—for just a few dollars—and bring it out disguised. Like Yi Dynasty white ware disguised as a chili paste container or Goryeo celadon with sesame oil inside.

"Even if it's not famous celadon or white ware, the kilns up here seem to have produced quite a few good things because there's lots of good clay in North Korea. There's even a blue glaze with unique characteristics like the ceramics from the Mt. Gyeryong area in the South. Where was it, again? I think it was somewhere in Hamgyeong Province.

"And there are lots of old paintings, calligraphy, and books circulating privately that aren't designated as cultural treasures or protected by the government. They'll fetch a pile of money in South Korea. That thief said he got a painting by a great artist like Gyeomje or Danwon for a thousand dollars—and that's being generous—and sold it in Seoul for hundreds of millions of *won*. He once traded an old metal printing plate for an electric rice cooker—some Buddhist scripture, I think—and sold it in Seoul for hundreds of millions."

"But an ancient scroll or a printing plate—those should have been immediately recognized. . . ."

"Customs on the China–North Korea border isn't very thorough. They're lax about antiques that aren't designated cultural treasures, and the dollar goes a long way with the officials."

It was clear now, without my having to ask any more questions: the amazing power of the capitalist enterprise had already penetrated this far. Then Mr. Reunification let loose with something else.

"They say you can't keep an old dog down, right? On top of all this, he's keeping a wife just for here." The twisted smile on his face suggested that this was what he really wanted to talk about, and though I knew it wasn't proper, I couldn't help but ask, "What did you say?"

"He has a Korean Chinese girl who acts as a go-between. He must have pumped her with thousands of dollars—she's shameless. She acts like she's his wife even in front of me. He told me he used her as a personal translator and secretary when he first came up here on business. I wouldn't mind that much if he was messing with a Han Chinese, but a Korean girl—that's like incest! Last night they went out together and didn't come back. I saw her come in again as I left for lunch today, and now the two of them are in there giggling."

It chilled me, the power of money to transform anything into a commodity, but now that I had been recognized, it wasn't a subject I could dwell on. By then we'd emptied three bottles of Tsingtao beer between us, and I'd already had quite a few drinks earlier in the day, but I still retained a degree of discretion. He seemed to have a lot more to say, but I changed the subject and asked him a question to get him to stop. "So, how is the reunification work going?"

I was just repeating the phrase I'd heard from the businessman, but Mr. Reunification seemed to detect some sarcasm in the phrase. He immediately became defensive.

"I knew you'd met up with that grave robber, but you must have heard something. I don't have the ability or the qualifications for it to be called 'reunification work.' What exactly did he tell you?"

"Nothing, really. The work you do—that's pretty much it, isn't it? I was just using a convenient phrase, but if it offended you, I apologize."

Mr. Reunification didn't take issue with me after that. I got the feeling that he was upset not because of any sarcasm in my remark, but because it reminded him of something else.

"You don't need to apologize. . . . I've been meeting with people here and there in case it might help the cause, but the results haven't been that great. I should have just gone to see the lake at Mt. Baekdu."

"It didn't look to me like you intended to go to Mt. Baekdu in the first place," I said casually, but this seemed to be no small shock to Mr. Reunification.

He tried hard to conceal his uneasiness as he explained. "I thought you wouldn't notice, since you're an academic, but you have sharp eyes. I've got nothing to hide. Actually, the organization I've belonged to for many years is disbanding. We're in the process of creating a reunification movement that reaches beyond just Korea. We're focusing on Yanji for its geopolitical location, and we're hanging a lot of hope on the Koreans here. You might say I'm here as a special envoy. My job is meeting with supporters who have maintained ties with us from before, and finding useful people.

"The reason I hid in a tour group was because I didn't want to attract unwanted attention. It's not necessary for those who go to America, but the person who went to Russia also went in a tour group to Moscow and the Tashkent area. . . . I've met and spoken with a lot of people in the past two days, but our goals don't seem to be as widely understood as we thought."

"Is it possible that your approach is wrong? Taking a purely political approach to reunification . . ." I'm sure I was drunk by then. I had blurted out something that couldn't be said so simply, again repeating something I'd heard the previous day from the businessman.

But the alcohol was having its effect on Mr. Reunification, too. His reaction was unexpectedly fierce.

"You mean the theory that economic problems have to take priority? Or that a plan for reunification that neglects economic considerations is just naïve sentimentality? Are you one of them, Professor? Well, you'd better keep this straight. Those bastards who consider economics or anything else top priority when they talk about reunification—they're nothing but con men. Or ultra-right-wing reactionaries who are pushing for reunification just so South Korea can absorb the North."

Perhaps he thought he was being too harsh, because he continued only after he had calmed down a bit.

"Reunification is only natural and right. It's rejoining a people who were originally one. It's a land that was originally one nation returning to being one nation. To say such a goal is political, or to prioritize other things like economic considerations or cultural homogeneity—that's just disguised anti-reunification rhetoric.

"They say they're being rational, or prudent, but they have other motives. The ones who put economic matters first are especially evil, even worse than the ones who want reunification through absorption. They're actually imperialists at heart. They look at reunification as a way of acquiring a colony the size of North Korea, or as a way to double the market and get twenty million new consumers. If that's not the case, why are the economic conditions in the North and the affluence of the South so important to them? If they consider North Koreans and us as one bloodline and one family, why bring up nonsense like reunification expenses? Isn't sharing everything— have or have not—what blood relations do?"

"I'm not sure," I said. "In today's world even brothers born from the same mother don't always share everything. The Germans planned carefully for decades before the Wall came down, but they're going through rough times now. And Yemen decided to unify politically first, but now they're in the middle of a bloody north-south civil war. . . ."

I had said something else thing to the businessman the previous day. This time I tried subtly supporting the economy-centered reunification theory. It was an easy about-face because I'd never been seriously engaged in the reunification debate. And just as I had expected, it got Mr. Reunification fired up again.

"That's exactly the kind of nonsense I'm talking about," he said. "Look at it this way. How realistic is it, the fantasy that seventy million from North and South will come together joyfully, in unanimous agreement, because they're all economically secure, everything's equal, and so they have nothing to lose and are part of the same culture in the first place? Do you think they promote that scenario because they really think that day will come? I mean, people who spout that nonsense are more calculating—they're a lot shrewder than we are and they know that day will never come. Instead of such a transparent con, isn't it better to just reunify and worry about all the fallout afterward? At least that's honest. Isn't it, Professor?"

Well, I could have posed some questions—perhaps about the possibility of another Korean War being sparked by the problems of reunification—but I was suddenly very tired. I have to confess that I have something like a guilt complex about engaging in any kind of ideological argument—not just about reunification. It might be my self-consciousness because of my father's defection to the North, or maybe it's the idea of original sin, amplified by rigorous anticommunist indoctrination when I was a child. In any case, whenever I get into ideological arguments, I immediately become exhausted. So I tried to sidestep the issue, but only ended up causing more trouble.

"Actually, I'm not saying that I'm opposed to an approach that puts politics first . . . ," I said. "I was just repeating something I heard from someone. On the off chance that it might be useful to you."

I wasn't only thinking about what the businessman had said in the coffee shop the previous day, but Mr. Reunification quickly figured out who that "someone" was. His face grew so red it clearly wasn't just from the alcohol.

"That's what that thieving rat said, isn't it?" he asked loudly. "He spouted cynical stuff like that yesterday, too. That's exactly it. Guys like him pretend they're the only people in the world who know anything about anything. Whenever talk of reunification comes up, they don't care what state the economy is in or whether we should think things through—they end up confusing even good, intelligent people. Like they say, it's whores for foreigners who walk first when a new road gets built. As soon as Yanji opened up, it was those kinds of thieving bastards who went in and out, corrupting the innocent Korean people here. They gave them a taste for money, got them used to it as they lured and cheated them. Now they're all chasing after money, money, money, shoving their own people and ideology out of the way. And if that's not enough, that bastard started doing it on the North Korean side, too. He's smuggling out antiques one at a time now, but do you know what would happen if we reunified by absorbing North Korea? All the real estate belonging to the North Koreans who don't understand the idea of private property will end up in the hands of bastards like him for pennies—give it three months! They don't think twice about exploiting North Korea's economic problems for usury or human trafficking. It won't be anything to scoff at, either. They'll do things more terrible to the land than what the Japanese did during the occupation. They claim the North Koreans are defacing nature by carving the names of Kim Il Sung and Kim Jong Il on boulders on the mountainside, but if you give those bastards free rein, that will all pale by comparison. Beautiful places like the Diamond Mountains and Mt. Myohyang will be trashed by motels and private villas where they'll shack up with their young girls. If we want to achieve anything, we have to purge those bastards first—before reunification."

There are some people in this world who simply do not suit each other. They have the uncanny ability to zero in on each other's weaknesses and faults and, oddly enough, they cannot leave each other alone. Mr. Reunification and the businessman seemed to have exactly that kind of relationship. They hadn't known each other before this trip as far as I could tell, and had only shared a room for two nights, but Mr. Reunification spoke as if the businessman was his lifelong enemy.

Regardless of who was right or wrong, I was in an uncomfortable position. After diplomatically supporting both sides in order to cover myself, I finally escaped from Mr. Reunification at around six o'clock.

Resisting the urge to go drink myself into a stupor and pass out somewhere, I went back to my room. I still needed to settle up with Mr. Kim, and it was possible that my brother would come by again. And getting drunk would certainly make moving on to Beijing difficult.

It was the right decision. Mr. Kim knocked on my door less than half an hour later. Settling our account went very smoothly. Maybe it was his first time, as he had said, but he didn't pad his figures. Even after I added the twenty thousand yuan tip I had already decided to give him on top of his fee, the total wasn't much more than I had anticipated.

So I ended up with more dollars than I expected, and that made me think of my brother again. I had planned to use up all of those dollars, so I decided to give them to him if he came back. I even tried coming up with a rationale. *Take this—you paid the expenses for Father's funeral, which I should have rightly paid as his first son, if I had been taking care of him. Take this—it might be useful if news gets out about our meeting and causes you problems.* But what Mr. Kim said put a damper on my plan.

"I think it will be hard for your brother to come back. The Korean middlemen around here are full of themselves these days because of all the people escaping from North Korea. They can get a reward for just reporting them to the Chinese. They have them rounded up and sent back to North Korea.

"And there are North Korean special agents with fire in their eyes who sneak across the border to hunt down those people. Just be glad you could spend that much time with your brother. It's best to keep these things short—he should just spend a few days with his uncle, pick up some things he needs and go back home."

But my brother did come back. . . . I had finished dinner with the rest of the group, who had returned from Mt. Baekdu after 8:00 p.m. About an hour later, I was in the middle of a shower, getting ready for the rest of my trip— washing away the alcohol I had drunk here and there during the course of the day—when someone pounded on my door. I hurriedly dried off and opened the door to find my brother standing outside, obviously drunk.

"Brother," he said. "It's me. There's more I have to tell you."

I quickly let him in and closed the window I had left open for some air. When he saw me checking to make sure the door was fully closed, he noticed my anxiety even in his drunken state.

"Don't worry, brother!" he said loudly. "I planned everything. In advance. There's nothing to worry about, even if special agents from National Security show up. Give me something to drink, if you have anything."

I sat him down, and opened the door of the small refrigerator. Unlike the hotel I'd stayed in two years ago, this one stocked quite a few varieties of liquor. My brother wanted something strong, so I grabbed a small bottle of whisky and a couple bags of dry snacks.

"So what is it you want to tell me?" I asked.

He downed the whiskey I poured him in a single gulp, not even bothering to add ice. "There's a lot. Lots of hate, lots of heartache, lots of regret . . ." he said plaintively. He sniffled once, then let it all pour out like someone whose dam had burst.

"Brother, do you know what you were to me until I met you in person? Father only told me about you just before he died, but I knew about you for a long time. I'd be alone with Father in the yard and I'd get a strange feeling from the way he looked at me. There was affection, but it also felt like he was looking at someone else, behind me. . . . When I was little, I didn't know who that was, but I figured it out when I got older—it was obviously you.

"And there's more. I mean, the feeling that I was constantly being compared to someone else. Father would praise me when I brought home tests or report cards that I thought were pretty good, but there were times when he'd look up at the empty sky—ever so briefly—and be lost in thought. That's when he was comparing me with someone else. In his blank eyes, there were someone else's tests and report cards. I figured out who it was before I got to middle school."

I faintly recalled the test sheets and report cards from my childhood. Of course. My grades from the first year of elementary school—when Father stayed in the countryside close to Seoul so he could hide with us—were brilliant. Once, when I had brought home perfect scores ten times in a row, Father rubbed his stubbly chin on my cheek so hard it made me scream. I always got five concentric red circles on my homework, the highest mark. . . .

But after that one year, my grades never regained their former glory. As the oldest son of a single mother struggling to make a living and moving from place to place with three young children, I was left back a grade every couple of years and couldn't even attend school for months at a time between moves. It was nearly impossible to maintain good grades, no matter how hard I tried.

"There's more," said my brother. "There aren't many people who worked as hard as Father did all his life. I can't remember ever seeing him in bed, except when he was dying. From the time I was a kid, Father was already gone to the work site and nowhere to be seen by the time I opened my eyes in the morning. And when I was on my way to bed, he was always reading something, like he had no intention of ever sleeping.

"I've never met anyone who knew as much as Father. There was no question he couldn't answer, no matter what I asked him about—science, math, history—right up until I graduated from college. That's why we never went hungry, you know. But as I got older and wiser, I did begin to wonder. Why couldn't we live better when Father worked so hard? I mean, father was so smart that Mother—she was smart herself, and from a good family—fell in love and married him when she was so much younger. Why did he have to kowtow to the Party leaders? The answer was pretty obvious.

"We knew. Even if we went to Kim Il Sung University, we wouldn't be able to get into the political science department or international relations. If we joined the army, there was no way we could ever become officers. And we figured out that we shouldn't even consider becoming a Party official or National Security agent, let alone apply for the Ministry of Social Welfare. We could see the unfair treatment our well-born and capable brother-in-law had to face for marrying our sister. . . .

"It was because of Father's connection to the South—the blood tie, the one that can't be severed, even though you can cut everything else. Otherwise, Father's devotion and hard work would have easily gotten him past the Party's suspicion of intellectuals who came from the South. To us, you and your family in the South weren't so much blood relations as an invisible curse—a disaster. . . ."

I was momentarily dumbstruck. What a strange reversal! I found it hard to believe that—though the methods were different—my brother in the North had suffered the same discrimination and stigma of guilt by association that I had suffered in the South. And his vivid though poorly drawn image of me—it was exactly that kind of image of Father that I had carried with me in my youth. Could my siblings really have seen me that way? Father had become a curse to me because of a willful choice on his part, but what choice had I had in my own life? From early on I had vaguely experienced, firsthand, the insignificance of a single individual's choice in the vast canvas of history, but once I heard my brother's pointed complaints, I was speechless. It was a shock for me to understand the clot of resentment in my brother's heart.

"Do you know what I was thinking when I left to come here? Frankly, it had nothing to do with Father's dying wish. That only made me strangely jealous. Why did he want me to give you the highest award he ever received? What were you to us, anyway? I came here because I was curious about you, not to carry out Father's last request. I couldn't resist coming to see what our long curse looked like in person. No—it was more than that. It was like setting out to find my lifelong nemesis. . . .

"But the instant I laid eyes on you, that wasn't it. I can't really explain it, but from the moment we met, you weren't my nemesis. You were just my brother. I mean—you're someone to embrace, to cry with, not someone to curse and hate. I mean—as time went by, all the hatred I brought with me turned into shame. I even had the illusion that you were someone I had missed for such a long time. . . .

"So what happened here? Tell me! Where can you go to satisfy your lifelong grudge, and where can we go to satisfy ours? Something went wrong here. What happened? Can you tell me, brother? What really happened here?"

I don't know, either, brother. The truth is I share the futility and emptiness you feel—they were in the tears I shed by the Tumen River. All I know is that an era has passed, that the time has come for me to find some way to change my view of life. I am beginning to feel that though life may be full of cruelty and suffering, I cannot pass on the blame—for any of it—to anyone else.

"I told you lots of lies. When I said I was on the Gimchaek Enterprise Consortium Party Committee, that was a complete lie. I'd like to be on that committee, but that's not where I actually work. The mine where I work is overseen by Gimchaek Consolidated Industries, but I'm only an ore technician who sorts gravel. My younger sister who married a leader in the Light Industries Committee? It's true, but he's a widower, much older than me. With two kids from his previous wife. She was such a proper and smart girl, but it's only because he was a widower that she could marry a comrade with such a high position. . . . The youngest who went to Pyongyang Foreign Language College—he's a bright kid, too. He dreamed about getting into the political science department at Kim Il Sung University, but that was the best he could do. Father, too. He spent his whole life going up and down, working in a respectable research position or at a tough worksite, always insecure until the end. 'A man who received more than he gave for the nation'—that's a cliché from pop song lyrics up here in the North. The truth is, Father suffered a lot until the moment he died.

"We got hold of painkillers through Uncle Gyeongho with what we saved here and there, but for the last three days we couldn't even do that. We just had to watch Father suffering, twisting around in pain."

Brother, I don't want to hear any more of this—for your sake. You still have to live under that system for a while. If the shoes don't fit, you have to make your feet fit the shoes. The progressives in the South criticize my pessimism, but I urge you, amicably, because you are my flesh and blood. You know the present is not ideal, but don't let that make you impatient for an unrealistic future. Don't be tempted by a revolution without thinking through the consequences. The time will come.

"I lied about my older sister, too. The vice secretary of the International Economics Bureau I mentioned earlier—actually, he's not a friend, he's my brother-in-law. He fell in love with my sister in college and married her despite all the problems it caused in his career. He's a graduate of the College of International Relations at Kim Il Sung University and he's nearly fifty, but he's still only a vice secretary—in the Economic Bureau. He's in Beijing now, with my sister. At the family meeting before I left, it was decided that we shouldn't tell you about Big Sister. We thought if you went looking for her impulsively, it wouldn't be good for my sister or her husband. But don't worry. Here's her phone number. Meet her in Beijing if you have the time. Brother and sister meeting each other—what harm could that do?"

My brother handed me a piece of paper with a phone number written on it, then he passed out. My room had twin beds, so I dragged him to the spare bed and lay him down. As I took off his clothes, I noticed his pitiful suit—probably his first, the best one he could get so as not to embarrass himself.

I stayed up very late thinking, unable to sleep, but still woke early the next morning. When I looked over at my brother's bed, I saw that he had kicked aside the blanket I'd tucked around him in the night. He was curled up like a shrimp, sleeping in the fetal position. I got up quietly and covered him again with the blanket that was bunched in the corner. My brother stirred and woke up as I was straightening his pillow.

Unlike the night before, when the drinking had made him loud, he was very self-conscious and hastily put on his clothes. I thought it might be best for him to leave the hotel before it was completely light out, so instead of stopping him I presented him with the envelope I'd prepared during the night.

"Take this. It's $2,600. You might be able to use it." That was all I said. I didn't think I needed a pretext for giving it to him.

My brother hesitated and stared at me. I thought he was going to say something, but then he changed his mind and politely took the envelope in both hands.

"Thank you, big brother," he said. "Then goodbye." He bowed his head like a schoolboy and left the room.

This may be an unnecessary addendum, but I feel I must tell the rest of what happened in Beijing. My decision to meet my younger sister—something I'd never thought of—was born from the meeting with my brother, and the argument I witnessed between Mr. Reunification and the businessman was a sort of extension of my meeting with my brother. Perhaps that's what reunification is, only on a grander scale and all at once: meeting a brother whose face you've never seen.

We landed in Beijing around one in the afternoon that day. As soon as my hotel room was assigned, I dialed the number my brother had given me. A young woman answered the phone, and when I gave my sister's name, she curtly told me that she was out. Her voice was so hard and cold that I hesitated a little, but then I left my name and the number of my hotel room, asking her to have my sister call me when she returned.

I waited by the phone all afternoon, but the phone call from my sister never came. I grew tired of waiting and I tried calling again, around dinnertime. The same young woman answered and gave me the same response. And it was the same again after that. I called again that night and then the following morning, but each time the same woman picked up and gave the same answer, as if she'd been waiting by the phone.

Eventually, it was checkout time at the hotel. The rest of the group left for a tour of the Thirteen Tombs of the Ming emperors and I was the only one left. It was almost noon, and I wouldn't be able to stay in the room much longer. I hurriedly dialed the number one last time. Suddenly it occurred to me that her voice had sounded oddly familiar. It was the voice of my older sister in Taegu, in her younger days. . . . Just then, the woman's voice came through the receiver, and as I listened it sounded more and more like my older sister. *It was you*, I thought. *It was because I figured that you were forty years old, because I expected the voice of a middle-aged woman, that I didn't notice the similarity in your voices.*

I wondered why my sister could only answer my calls that way. Maybe she had heard from my brother, and she'd been warned that I would call her. She might have some reason—which she could not tell me—for not being able to meet me and had been waiting nervously by the phone to turn me away. I paused at that point. Why must I insist on meeting her if she had reason to avoid me? I had done nothing for her as an older brother—was it right to stubbornly press for a meeting that might be harmful to her? Yet it was hard to turn back, having come so close. I came up with a lukewarm compromise. Convinced that she was Munhui, I tried to convey my message to her in a roundabout way.

"When Ms. Munhui returns, please tell her that her brother from the South called and wanted to meet her. I leave on a four o'clock flight for Seoul, and I don't know if I'll be able to visit the North again, so I'll be very disappointed if I don't get to see her. If I did manage to return, there's no way of knowing if she will still be here. . . . But I'll be here in the hotel lobby until one, and then after two o'clock, I'll be at the airport. So if by chance she returns before then, could you please tell her?"

"I understand," she said after a short pause. "I'll make sure to give her the message when she comes back. Then . . . have a good trip." Maybe I imagined it, but I thought I heard a quaver in her voice at the very end, during the goodbye.

Afterward, I waited in the hotel lobby for two hours, then another hour at the airport, but Munhui never came. That last goodbye over the phone had been her farewell.

I had finally given up and had turned my gaze from the airport entrance to the place where our tour group was gathered when the businessman approached. He hovered over me for a while before asking, cautiously, "Professor, could you do me a favor?"

I didn't answer, still preoccupied with my thoughts. When I finally gave him a questioning look, he handed me two long cardboard tubes that looked like they might contain pictures.

"Since you don't have much luggage, would you mind carrying these for me until we get to Seoul?"

They were cardboard tubes that contained scrolls, the kind everyone bought in tourist shops before coming back from a trip to China. When I looked at him quizzically, as if to ask why he needed me to carry such commonplace items, he smiled awkwardly.

"I'll be honest with you. The tubes aren't much, but the pictures inside are old. Have you ever heard the pen name Yosujae?"

"Yosujae? It's the first time I've heard that name."

"He was a landscape painter from the late Joseon period. He's not as well known as Danwon or Hyewon, but his brushwork and his use of color are fantastic. These tubes have a couple of his paintings in them." He gave me a conspiratorial wink, as if to confirm that I understood his intention.

I took the tubes reluctantly—I felt I couldn't refuse—and went to look around the waiting area, where something drew my attention. It was Mr. Reunification sitting quietly in a chair in a corner while others from the group were marching about like they owned the place. He looked depressed, lost in thought, despondent about something.

The businessman was still hovering around me. "It's no surprise," he whispered when he noticed where I was looking.

"He went around with his big talk, making empty promises, and he got cut down to size. I heard it was a Korean from Yanji who did it. He'd been taken by somebody like Mr. Reunification before. He treated the guy to food and drink for days, and then, when the guy went home, he didn't even get a 'How are you?' letter, let alone an invitation to Seoul. They say Mr. Reunification was getting so worked up with his speech that he didn't notice how people were reacting. The man—he got up without warning and dumped the whole drinking table on him.

"It may seem like a terrible bolt from the blue, but he really deserved it. He saw how the old Soviet bloc countries toppled one after the other in Eastern Europe—how could he just spout that empty rhetoric? I knew he would get himself into trouble like that. . . ."

I remembered the stains I had seen on Mr. Reunification's suit the previous day in Yanji, but for some reason I was in no mood to make light of his failure. The businessman's gleeful laugh made me sick, and I turned away. Just then, the travel agency worker appeared, wiping the sweat on his forehead, and yelled out to us.

"Boarding starts in five minutes! Please collect your documents!"

In his left hand he was still clutching the stack of passports he had gathered together for safekeeping—afraid they might be stolen, or lost.

(*continued from page ii*)

The Columbia Anthology of Modern Chinese Drama, edited by Xiaomei Chen
(2011)

Qian Zhongshu, *Humans, Beasts, and Ghosts: Stories and Essays*, edited by
Christopher G. Rea, translated by Dennis T. Hu, Nathan K. Mao, Yiran
Mao, Christopher G. Rea, and Philip F. Williams (2011)

Dung Kai-cheung, *Atlas: The Archaeology of an Imaginary City*, translated by
Dung Kai-cheung, Anders Hansson, and Bonnie S. McDougall (2012)

O Chŏnghŭi, *River of Fire and Other Stories*, translated by Bruce Fulton and
Ju-Chan Fulton (2012)

Endō Shūsaku, *Kiku's Prayer: A Novel*, translated by Van Gessel (2013)

Li Rui, *Trees Without Wind: A Novel*, translated by John Balcom (2013)

Abe Kōbō, *The Frontier Within: Essays by Abe Kōbō*, edited, translated, and with
an introduction by Richard F. Calichman (2013)

Zhu Wen, *The Matchmaker, the Apprentice, and the Football Fan: More Stories of
China*, translated by Julia Lovell (2013)

The Columbia Anthology of Modern Chinese Drama, Abridged Edition, edited by
Xiaomei Chen (2013)

Natsume Sōseki, *Light and Dark*, translated by John Nathan (2013)

Seirai Yūichi, *Ground Zero, Nagasaki: Stories*, translated by Paul Warham (2015)

Hideo Furukawa, *Horses, Horses, in the End the Light Remains Pure: A Tale That
Begins with Fukushima* (2016)

Abe Kōbō, *Beasts Head for Home: A Novel*, translated by Richard F. Calichman
(2017)

HISTORY, SOCIETY, AND CULTURE
Carol Gluck, Editor

Takeuchi Yoshimi, *What Is Modernity? Writings of Takeuchi Yoshimi*, edited and
translated, with an introduction, by Richard F. Calichman (2005)

Contemporary Japanese Thought, edited and translated by Richard F. Calichman
(2005)

Overcoming Modernity, edited and translated by Richard F. Calichman (2008)

Natsume Sōseki, *Theory of Literature and Other Critical Writings*, edited and
translated by Michael Bourdaghs, Atsuko Ueda, and Joseph A. Murphy (2009)

Kojin Karatani, *History and Repetition*, edited by Seiji M. Lippit (2012)

The Birth of Chinese Feminism: Essential Texts in Transnational Theory, edited by
Lydia H. Liu, Rebecca E. Karl, and Dorothy Ko (2013)

Yoshiaki Yoshimi, *Grassroots Fascism: The War Experience of the Japanese People*,
translated by Ethan Mark (2015)